Alive and Unharmed

by

Crystal Hubbard

East Baton Rouge Parish Library
Baton Rouge, Louisiana

Moxie is an imprint of Parker Publishing Inc

Copyright © 2013 by Crystal Hubbard
Published by Parker Publishing Inc
12523 Limonite Avenue, Suite #440-438
Mira Loma, California 91752
www.parker-publishing.com

ISBN: 978-1-60043-144-9 (print)
First Edition

Manufactured in the United States of America
Cover Design by Parker Publishing Inc

This novel is dedicated to Melanie Ann, who brightens every darkness…

Chapter One

Reece Wyndham followed the sloping curves of the driveway leading to the Holland brick mansion at its end. A twinge of unease made the flesh at the back of her neck bristle, and she gripped the strap of her backpack a little tighter.

"What am I doing here?" she muttered with a giggle of disbelief. *Delivering Christopher's American Literature review sheets, that's what,* she answered herself, steeling her resolve. *And if Logan Maddox's Labor Day party happens to come up, and Christopher needs a date, then maybe this errand will be worthwhile for both of us.*

Christopher August Daley III lived in Adler, the suburb for the super-rich surrounding Prescott High School. Reece lived three miles farther southeast, in the working-class town of Brentwood. The driveways in her neighborhood featured garden center lawn gnomes, not stone fountains spouting jewel-blue water in seven directions. She passed the front gates of the Daley estate every day when she ran to and from school, never dreaming that she would one day darken its ornately carved double doors.

She inhaled deeply, certain she detected the scent of money as she neared Christopher's house.

Christopher's *palace.*

"They're going to release the hounds on me or something," she mused. She felt so grossly out of place as her running shoes moved soundlessly along the smooth black driveway. The Wyndhams weren't exactly paupers, but compared to the comfortable old money of the Daleys, Oprah Winfrey was poor and Bill Gates merely doing well. "What the – ?"

Reece's feet stopped along with her words. Two hooded figures carried a limp body—Christopher's body—through the wide doors of the mansion and down the marble stairs. They tossed him into the back of a van partially hidden by the huge fountain. The two men climbed in after Christopher. A few seconds later, the van skidded into motion, its tires spinning.

Reece, the star of Prescott's girls' track team, followed her instincts. She turned and ran, racing back the way she'd come, toward the sky-high black iron gates gaping open at the vast mouth of the estate. A Mercedes limousine and a chauffeur-driven Bentley moving in opposite directions passed the mouth of the driveway. Reece sprinted for them, shouting for help and waving her arms, hoping to flag down one of the ritzy autos.

The van sped up, passing her.

"Oh, crap!" she swore, horrified. The van angled in front of her and screeched to a halt, blocking her escape. She spun and ran back toward the mansion, shrugging her shoulder free of her heavy backpack. Unburdened, she accelerated, calling on three years of excellent training on the Prescott track.

A few yards from a low stone wall on the north side of the driveway, the van's rear doors opened and a man leaped out. He landed on Reece, forcing her to the hard surface of the driveway with his knee in her back.

Her first scream was one of anger, surprise and indignation. This was the first race she had ever lost. Her second scream was one of pain, a needle had entered the hard muscle of her upper thigh.

She didn't scream again.

"Reece!"

Someone called her name, someone angry. She was surprised to hear anything at all through the cotton that seemed to be packing her skull.

"Reece, come on. Wake up!"

That voice again. Deep. Male. Urgent.

"Damn it, Reece, get up!"

Pain, fresh and sharp, bloomed in the center of first one cheek then the other. *Hey!* she tried to protest, but the word was no more than a rasp of air. She opened her eyes.

Were they open? She blinked, seeing only black. She threw a hand into the darkness.

"That's good," the voice encouraged. "Come on, hit me, if you can find me."

She was pulled into a sitting position. Waves of nausea

crested within her head and slammed violently against the walls of her gut. Her stomach knotted and she keeled onto her side, her arms clasped about her middle.

What's happening to me? she wondered pitifully, the bitter heat of bile burning the back of her throat.

A hand came to rest on her forehead and she batted at it. Someone hoisted her up by her armpits and onto her feet.

"Come on, you have to move." The bossy voice had a body after all. She relied on it to hold her up since her knees refused to cooperate.

"You have to move, Reece. You were doped."

Drugs? In her whole life she'd never taken anything stronger than over the counter headache pills. Her mystery date waltzed her across the uneven floorboards, which wasn't easy considering her bones seemed to have been replaced by wet noodles.

"You're supposed to be this great runner," he grunted. "You can't even walk."

I am a great runner! sounded in her head.

Her stomach lurched and she retched over his shoulder. A moment later, on her knees at the cool porcelain bowl of a toilet, she gave up the scant contents of her stomach, dry-heaving until her abdominal muscles cramped. Slumping over the toilet, she pressed a clammy hand to her forehead. "What's happening to me?" she moaned.

"Are you finished?"

She nodded weakly. "I can't see. Everything is shadowed and blurry."

"It'll pass. The lights don't work and the windows are boarded up. There's a little light coming in through the air vent, not that there's anything worth seeing. Are you finished?"

"I think so. You can let go of me now."

The arms supporting her vanished, but she wanted them back immediately. She wanted to rinse her mouth and wash her hands but she didn't trust her legs to carry her to the sink, wherever it was in the darkness.

"Where am I?" she asked.

"I don't know."
"Who did this to me?"
"I don't know."
"Who are you?"
"Christopher Daley. I've been kidnapped."

Whether she passed out because of his answer to her last question or the drug that had been used to subdue her, Christopher didn't know. At least she had fallen on him instead of the hard tile beneath his knees.

Hours ago, or what seemed like hours, he had awakened in the back of a fast-moving van. He had been nauseous and a little dull in the head at first, but the sensations quickly passed once he sat up and moved around a little. When the van stopped, two hooded men opened the back doors and forced him at gunpoint to the dark room on the second floor of a dilapidated house that smelled of wet leaves and damp animal fur. Reece had been carried in a few minutes later and dumped on the floor like a sack of garbage.

He could barely see her in the gloom of the sunset, its dark purple light bleeding into the long, narrow bathroom through the louvers of the air vent above the toilet. He'd been desperate for fresh air and had managed to pull off two of the boards nailed over the air vent. Gazing at the thread of fading light, he knew better than to hope his parents had noticed him missing. They had a full Labor Day weekend. Social events would keep them busy until work beckoned Tuesday morning. Lightly touching Reece's short dark hair, he hoped her parents or one of her sisters had noticed her missing. Unless his abductors had already contacted his father, his only hope of rescue lay with the unconscious girl in his lap.

The door burst open, the sudden light coming with it stinging Christopher's eyes. He stepped back as the two men thundered into the room. They were the same men who had who had broken down his bedroom door, wrestled him to the floor and jabbed a needle into his backside. The first man, the bigger of the two, grabbed a handful of Christopher's T-shirt and slammed him against the nearest wall.

He spoke directly into Christopher's face. "Keep bangin' on the door, you li'l jerk, and ah'll nail your damn hands to the wall," he growled through the black hood covering his head.

"She isn't well," Christopher said. He didn't back down even though his feet barely touched the floor. "She needs a doctor."

The big man released Christopher and went to Reece while his partner stood in the doorway, barring any attempt Christopher might have made to escape. The smaller man was about Christopher's size, but the gun clutched in his left hand gave him a distinct physical advantage.

The big man crossed the empty bedroom. "How much did you give her?" he asked over his shoulder.

"Same as him," the smaller man said anxiously, tipping his head toward Christopher.

Christopher's eyes adjusted to the light, and he wished for darkness again. Uneven floorboards, warped and splintered, matched the walls where chunks of plaster had fallen to expose bare wooden support beams. Water-stained wallpaper hung in dismal sheets from other parts of the walls. Judging from the thick ropes of dusty cobwebs suspended from the bare ceiling, even the spiders had given up on the place.

The big man squatted over Reece, revealing a black gun tucked in the waistband of his grimy jeans. "He weighs more'n her," the big man snorted. "You gave 'er too much. She's overdosin'. This huckleberry is on the ride of 'er life. Or at the end of it."

The smaller man swallowed loudly. "I ain't had time to measure it out." Panic flavored the Ozark lilt of his speech. "She was gettin' away. No witnesses, 'member? Y'all said no witnesses."

The blood drained from Christopher's face. Most of the Daley house staff had gone home early for the holiday weekend.

Only Chester Bigelow, the estate manager, had been at the house when the kidnappers arrived. Bigelow had probably answered the door for them.

Please let him be alright, Christopher silently prayed. Bigelow was the stereotypical English house manager—prim, fussy and far too organized—and for thirteen years he'd been a major pain in Christopher's side. But the last thing Christopher wanted was for anything truly bad to happen to him, or to Reece, just because he was the son of C. August Daley II.

"Sorry 'bout your girlfriend," the big man chuckled through his hood. "Cuz is gonna love this." With that, he and his accomplice left, returning them to the darkness.

"She's not my girlfriend," Christopher muttered at the locked door.

He didn't know Reece well at all, despite the fact that they had been classmates for the past three years, going on four. They ran in separate circles, no pun intended.

What is she doing in this dark and disgusting room with hooded men holding us prisoner? Christopher wondered.

Could she be involved in this?

She opened her eyes to a flat wall of darkness and sat up, splaying her fingers to feel into the black for the wall, or more preferably, the person who'd been so kind to her. Christopher Daley III, she recalled. He was there, somewhere.

"Chris?" The name barely penetrated the dark upon leaving the furry confines of her mouth. Her mouth tasted awful, and with embarrassment she remembered how it got that way. She found a wall and cautiously moved along it. "Are you here?" She stopped to calm the fear rising in her chest. Without her sight, her hearing seemed more acute. Faint breathing came from her left. "I know you're there." Her voice shook. "Please, answer me."

"You answer me."

"Chris?"

"Christopher." His name sliced through the dark with razor

sharpness.

She hesitated, listening. Was this still him? This voice was cold and brittle. The voice she'd heard before had been gentle and caring.

"Where are you?" she asked.

"You tell me."

"Chris, I—"

"Christopher," he snapped bitterly, "and cut the crap. Tell me who those men are and what they want."

Fear churned in her belly, and the queasiness hadn't entirely left her, but she wasn't going to let Chris—sorry, *Christopher*—bully her.

"How should I know?" Her voice swelled with tears and anger. "Mr. Huxhold asked me to bring you an American Literature review sheet for Tuesday's exam. I saw two men, in hoods…" She began to cry, recalling the cruelly vivid memory. "They carried you out of the house and put you into a van." An aftershock of nausea coursed through her and she had to sit down. Using the wall for support, she slid to the floor. "I tried to run. They caught me and shot me up with something. I woke up here with you. Wherever here is."

He weighed her story. She had been delivering schoolwork. That neatly explained why she was at his house after Friday's half day of classes. He was an idiot to have even suspected that she'd be in league with kidnappers. She had simply been in the wrong place at the absolute worst possible time.

It had to have been an inside job, surely orchestrated by someone who knew Daley Manor and the routine of its occupants. But, he hadn't told anyone that he'd planned to ditch his last class today. Or was it yesterday? His watch was gone so he had no idea of the time.

"I'm sorry," he mumbled.

"Me, too. I should have been able to help."

"I'll call ahead and warn you the next time I'm kidnapped. I'll expect you to be better prepared next time."

She didn't respond to his sarcasm. The darkness expanded in her silence, swallowing him whole. "It'll be all right," he said, softening his tone. "My father will pay whatever they ask. We'll be home in time for Saturday morning cartoons."

The eerie quiet made it harder for him to believe his own words. He listened more closely. She was crying. She did so quietly, but the sound touched his heart through his ears.

He went to her. "This is nothing to cry about."

"I'm not crying," she lied. Wyndham girls weren't crybabies. Sure, they cried at funerals and such, and Reece had cried an ocean after her father's accident, but tears never solved anything. This was the first time she had been so scared that she couldn't do anything *but* cry.

Christopher moved his hand through the darkness, until he found hers. "Tell me again what you saw."

She wiped her cheeks and her nose with the cuff of her sweatshirt. "They were in gray jumpsuits. They took you to a blue and white van. It had a cartoon vacuum riding a magic carpet on the side."

"Clever."

"I tried to get help. I tried to run for help."

His hand tightened around hers. "I'm sorry you got caught up in this."

"I want to go home," she blurted tearfully. She was scared, her throat was raw, she felt dirty and her palms were still stinging from her crash to the driveway. She desperately wanted out of this bad thing she had stumbled into. "My parents are probably worried to death. I have an exhibition race on Saturday and a date Sunday night." She clapped her hands to her face. "I want to go home!"

"Listen." He calmly took her hands. "I know you want to go home. You think I don't? We have to keep our heads. It's easy for me to say, I know. My parents have prepared me for this my whole life. Only I never really thought it would happen."

"Shows what you know," she sulked.

"My father will get us out of this. You'll see." He let go of her hands but remained close enough for his thigh to touch hers. "So who's the lucky guy?"

"What?"

"You said you had a date. With whom?"

"Logan Maddox."

"Really?"

"No." She laughed feebly. Logan Maddox, the star of a show called *Tom's Life*, had enrolled in their class. He had been at Prescott for two weeks and the school still hummed with the electricity of his superstar presence.

"The date isn't actually with Logan," she clarified. "It's Logan's party. He invited pretty much all of the senior class."

"When is it?"

"Sunday night. Since we have Monday off for Labor Day." She paused. "You didn't know? I figured you'd be on the 'A' list."

"What 'A' list?"

"Oh, please. Prescott has more cliques than a pair of tap shoes. There's the scholarship kids, the well-off kids, the rich kids, the stinking rich kids, and now there's Logan Maddox, a stinking rich, obscenely famous kid. Those groups are subdivided into melvins, zeldas, jocks, debs, stoners, loners, psychos, bimbos, himbos, supermodels, total freaks of nature –"

"Wait a minute. As much as I'm enjoying your blanket stereotypes of our schoolmates, what's a melvin?"

"Felix Nayland," she explained by way of example. "He's, like, King Melvin."

"I see." He knew King Melvin—Felix—through the computer sciences department. "A melvin is a nerd?"

"A melvin is an Internet-addicted, Jolt cola-sucking, sunlight-fearing, super-nerd to the millionth degree."

"What clique do I belong to?"

"You're in your own clique, I guess. Like me."

"That's funny, coming from the queen of the female jocks."

"I am not," she protested. "The other girls don't have much to do with me, outside of track."

"They're jealous of you."

"Yeah, right," she laughed in disbelief.

"You're always surrounded by a drooling pack of guys at school. When you cut your hair, the next week ten girls came to school with their hair in the same style."

"Really?"

"You didn't notice?"

"No," she said. "Why would they do that? Siobhan Curran and Courtney Miller are the trendsetters, not me. Hey," she said suspiciously.

"Hay is for horses."

"What?"

"I had an English nanny who would say that every time I said, 'hey.'"

"Oh. Okay…"

"You were talking about Siobhan and Courtney and their perch on the fresh edge of fashion," he reminded her.

"Oh, yeah. You noticed my haircut?"

"Yes, but what has that got to do with Siobhan or Courtney?"

"Nothing. It's got to do with you." She was glad for the darkness. Talking to him was easier without the distraction of his indigo eyes and perfect smile. "How so?"

"Do you notice every little change in the girls at school?"

"Just the interesting ones."

"The interesting changes or the interesting girls?"

"Both."

"You think I'm interesting?"

"Very much so."

She waited until she was sure she could speak in a normal tone before she said, "I'll bet you say that to all the girls."

"Well, I don't. And, for all the success I'm having now, I won't ever say it again."

"Don't be mad, Chris."

"Christopher," he insisted, over-enunciating. "Not Chris. Christopher."

"Don't be mad, *Christopher*," she said, rolling his name out as sweetly and flatly as cookie dough.

"I'm not mad. It's just…this is too weird, like a bad dream."

"It's like when you know you're dreaming, but you can't wake up," she said. "You just lie there, moaning and twitching and—"

"You've had bad dreams?" That familiar softness crept into his voice.

She blinked hard against the darkness. "Yes. But this one beats them all."

Chapter Two

They sat in the dark, nervously talking about nothing and everything to avoid thinking about their predicament. When the light suddenly blinked on, its sudden brightness burned their eyes.

Reece shrank into the wall as three men filed into the room. Two of them wore black hoods. The other, who was smartly dressed in an expensive-looking business suit, boldly showed his face. Reece's eyes fully adjusted to the light to see him leering at her, as if he wanted to rip her flesh from her bones with his tiny, chemically-whitened teeth.

The well-dressed man slowly appraised Reece from head to toe, his smile growing toothier as he took in the long, lean body beneath her faded jeans and baggy mulberry sweatshirt. Her brownish-black hair was boyishly short, but nothing else about her was boyish as she cowered at his feet. He was deciding which of her facial features was prettiest—the Cupid's bow of her mouth, the big honey-brown eyes that had grown larger in fear, or her dark bronze complexion—when he heard his name.

"Leighton Oliver," Christopher sneered, standing.

Oliver crossed his arms lazily over his chest. "I trust my cousins here handled you with kid gloves?" He knew full well they hadn't. The quality of their care showed on Christopher's face. He turned to the ill kempt pair behind him. "No need to hide the family resemblance. Christopher knows my name." He feigned horror. "Our charade is up."

Gentry Liggett, the smaller of the cousins, pulled off his hood and shook out thin locks of light brown hair styled in a choppy bowl cut. He didn't look much older than Christopher and Reece. He had fine, almost feminine features with long dark lashes framing his pale-as-water blue eyes. His thin lips disappeared when the left side of his mouth shot out in a crooked half smile. He tucked his hood into the back pocket of his tight-fitting jeans and then began picking at a mustard stain on the front of his threadbare T-shirt.

Ross Liggett took his time drawing the hood from his head,

exposing inch by inch the massive stump of his neck and thick locks of greasy brown hair grazing his heavily muscled shoulders. Above his wide fleshy nose, his eyes were small and pale, like dimes. He was as broad through the shoulders as Oliver and Gentry put together. He grinned, flashing four dead lower teeth and four gold-plated upper teeth.

"You ain't mad at us, fer brangin' 'er along?" Gentry said, hopefully.

"Men get angry. Dogs get mad," Oliver said dismissively, although he had been furious when Ross told him about the "li'l problem" in the abduction of Christopher August Daley III. Oliver had spent eight months planning the perfect crime, and suddenly he had two captives instead of one. At least the "li'l problem" was pleasing to the eye.

"Pretty, pretty," Oliver finally said. "I think we'll keep her."

A vein throbbed at Christopher's temple. "Reece has nothing to do with this."

"Oh, but she does," Oliver disagreed merrily, "though I wasn't aware you had a girlfriend. I've made it my business to be quite aware of you, Master Daley."

"She's not my girlfriend. I don't even know her."

Reece looked up at him, shocked and wounded, despite the truth of his words.

"Be that as it may, Christopher, she's now very much a part of this." Oliver was only an inch or two taller than Christopher. His impeccably tailored suit gave him the wide shoulders genetics had denied him.

Oliver turned to Reece. "What's your name?"

"Reece Wyndham," she whimpered.

"You're hardly the typical Prescott student. What is your father's name?"

"Craig Wyndham." Reece swiped a tear from her cheek.

"Of the Denver Wyndhams?"

"We're from Baltimore."

"And what does Craig Wyndham of Baltimore do for a living?"

"H-He's a fireman. Retired."

Oliver narrowed his eyes. "And your mother?"

"She teaches at Prescott."

"Ah," Oliver said with a knowing nod. "The children of Prescott faculty attend the school for free. In that case, you're worthless, Miss Wyndham."

"Do you have any idea how bad your life will be once my father catches you?" Christopher interjected. "You've worked for him long enough to know how he is. By this time tomorrow, I'll be in a hot tub with my Swiss masseuse and you'll be picking man pubes out of your teeth."

Oliver turned on him, his blue eyes livid. "It wouldn't be much different from what I do now," he sneered through clenched teeth, traces of his Ozark ancestry sneaking out, "which is kissing your old man's ass! I would've been just another Liggett, slaving fourteen hours a day at the fertilizer plant down in Juniper Falls alongside my cousins if I hadn't clawed my way out this hillbilly hell and got me a job at Daley International. Ten years I was with that company, and then your daddy went and hired out of the firm to fill the senior vice presidency. Ten years is a long time to wait for something that you know is yours! Your daddy owes me."

"What has that got to do with me?" Christopher spat. "Or her?" He jerked a thumb at Reece.

"You're my future," Oliver said simply. Every trace of the impassioned hillbilly vanished. "If your father is willing to buy you back, then you shall be returned to the cradle of luxury from which you were so carefully extracted."

"You're lying," Reece said tremulously. "You can't let us go. We've seen your face." She would never forget Oliver's empty blue eyes, his creepy teeth and the slick sheen of his light brown hair. "Christopher knows who you are."

"You've seen far too many movies, dear," Oliver said. "Once I collect the ransom from Augie Daley, I'll have the funds to vanish so completely, you'll wonder if I ever existed at all."

"Now who's seen too many movies," Christopher chuckled bitterly. "You won't get away with this. You think you've committed the perfect crime? You think you're getting some kind of sick revenge on my dad? If you really wanted to punish him, you should have left me at home. Idiot."

"Christopher, stop it," Reece cautioned, Oliver's expression darkening.

Christopher ignored her. "You and your cousins will wish you'd never been born before my dad finishes with you."

Oliver's right hand closed into a fist.

"Chris, don't," Reece whispered urgently.

"How long did you spend cooking up this little plan?" Christopher shook off Reece's desperate tug at his arm. "And, help me understand, you thought it was a *good* idea to recruit those two yahoos to help you? If they took Reece by mistake, God only knows what other stupid mistakes they've—"

Oliver's right hand smashed into Christopher's face. Reece cried out, nearly falling from her chair in fear. Christopher quietly knuckled away a thin trickle of blood from the corner of his mouth.

"Make no mistake about this, brat," Oliver sneered with cold calm. "You will do as you're told, your father will do as he's told, and your pretty friend here will do as she's told. Whether you live or die is up to your father and the two of you. It doesn't matter to me as long as I get paid."

"Whatever you're asking," Christopher said, "you'll repay double in skin."

"Be that as it may, Christopher." Oliver nonchalantly shook out his throbbing right hand. "In the meantime, we'd best prepare a message for your father." He crossed the room to confer with his cousins.

Reece got her first good look at Christopher's face. Purplish-black bruises bloomed on his left cheekbone and forehead; a fresh cut striped the slight swelling in his lower lip.

"Your face," she gasped, "your poor face. Those guys did this to you?"

"No, I did it to myself," he snarled.

"You don't have to be so obnoxious."

"Don't ask stupid questions and I won't be obnoxious."

"Children, stop squabbling," Oliver chided. "It's time for fun. We're going to make a movie."

Chapter Three

Craig Wyndham's fingers dug into the padded armrests of his chair. Christopher August Daley II had entered the house like an angry feudal lord, wearing an Italian suit that probably cost more than the Wyndham's earned in a month. Mrs. Daley – former supermodel Nicole Payton – wore a raw silk suit casual suit that matched her anxious blue-green eyes.

Craig and Sara Wyndham had been up all night worrying about Reece. She hadn't been seen since leaving school school early Friday afternoon. She was eighteen, so the police couldn't do anything to find her until twenty-four hours had elapsed. And now, an hour before sunrise, a Forbes-cover billionaire sat on their old sofa, staring at the platinum Rolex circling his wrist after telling them something completely inconceivable.

"I don't understand," Mr. Wyndham said, his voice tight with a fear he'd never known, even after twenty years as a firefighter.

Mr. Daley sighed impatiently. When he spoke, he did so slowly, as if trying to explain the dynamics of a corporate buyout to a first-grader. "Our son Christopher, and your daughter Racine, have been abducted," Mr. Daley said. "They have been *kidnapped*. Have you been contacted?"

Mrs. Wyndham cupped her elbows in her palms. The chill of the unseasonably cool September night penetrated her dark green chenille robe. "My daughter's name is Reece. And you think she's been abducted? We've called the school, all her friends, the police—"

"My wife and I were awakened two hours ago," Mr. Daley loudly cut in, grinding the heels of his leather uppers into the worn brown carpeting. "The kidnappers say they have Christopher and his girlfriend Rice, Racine or whatever her name is. They gave us this address and said their next contact would be here." He impatiently threaded his fingers through the distinguished silver at his temples. He leaned far off the sofa, hands wide, and his wife put a restraining hand on his knee. "We would have been here sooner, but we had to resolve a problem at the estate."

What they'd had to do was find Chester Bigelow, the estate manager, who had been beaten, bound, gagged, and stowed in a kitchen pantry.

"This is impossible." Mrs. Wyndham sank into the armchair near her husband. "This can't be happening." Her gaze darted from Mr. Daley to his wife.

"I'm afraid it is, Mrs. Wyndham," Mr. Daley said gravely.

"Sara," Mrs. Wyndham said weakly. "Please. Call me Sara."

"You're right," Mrs. Daley said, taking Sara's trembling hand. "This situation definitely calls for first names. I'm Nicole. My husband's friends call him Augie."

"We have to call the police again." Mr. Wyndham wheeled himself toward the kitchen. "Have you notified the authorities? What are they doing to find the children?"

Mr. Daley shot from the sofa and grabbed the back of Mr. Wyndham's wheelchair, stopping him. Mr. Wyndham spun around with a vicious glare.

"No police," Mr. Daley urged. "The man who contacted me was quite specific about that. Until we know who we're dealing with, it would be best to follow their instructions to the letter."

Mr. Wyndham glowered at him. "You come to my home at five in the morning, you tell me my daughter's been kidnapped, and you expect me to sit here and wait for a phone call? You might own half this city and most of the people in it, but you don't own me," he added mockingly, "Augie."

"Do you think these people won't hurt our children?" Mr. Daley asked. "Don't be naïve!"

"Augie, lower your voice," his wife told him. She glanced at the portrait displayed over the back of the sofa. "There are children sleeping in this house."

Mr. Daley followed Mr. Wyndham into the kitchen, where the two men argued in much lowered, but acidic tones.

"Would you like some coffee?" Mrs. Wyndham offered, a wan smile betraying her fear and anxiety through the mundane inquiry.

"That would be nice." Mrs. Daley hung back in the living

room while Mrs. Wyndham went to the kitchen. The noise of the argument raging inside escaped for a second when the door swung open.

The Wyndham house was just like the others lining each side of Rankin Avenue. Each ranch house had a carport and a wide driveway, and the same landscaping—if that's what you called a yew hedge and a blue spruce flanking the front door. Chevrolets and Fords, and an occasional late model Honda or Toyota, sat parked under the carports and on the street. The Daley's Jaguar stuck out like a cultured heirloom rose in a daisy patch.

The Wyndham home was furnished in what Mrs. Daley called "20th century hand-me-downs," the mass-produced, wood-laminate covered, particle-board antique-a-likes that newlyweds scavenged from the attics and garages of generous relatives to furnish their starter homes. The Wyndham starter home in Brentwood had clearly become their ancestral estate.

Wringing one hand anxiously over the other, Mrs. Daley wandered into the small dining room. She gazed at a centerpiece of silk roses in the middle of the drop-leaf table. The roses were pale shades of buttercream blue and ivory that didn't exist in nature. A bittersweet half-smile came to her face as she touched a faux petal.

Long before she hung up her supermodel stilettos and married a man fifteen years her senior, she had been Nicki Payton, the daughter of a nurse and a Greek deli owner. With a pang of nostalgia she recalled the number of meatloaf and mashed potatoes dinners she had eaten in the presence of a huge bouquet of artificial roses as she kicked her younger sister beneath a 20th-century hand-me-down dining table.

The argument in the kitchen grew louder with Mrs. Wyndham attempting to quiet the husbands. Mrs. Daley had no desire to add her stress and worry to that of the other three parents, so she retreated to the living room. The contents of a tall display case caught her attention. The unit was more than six feet tall and behind its glass doors sat trophies, ribbons, awards, medallions, certificates and other objects commemorating the achievements of the six Wyndham girls.

Taryn Wyndham had kicked and blocked her way to dozens of Tae Kwon Do championships. Reece had run away with a blizzard of blue ribbons and what could very well be her weight in shiny championship trophies and first-place medals. Bailey had aced victories in dozens of tennis tournaments. Kelsey, a dancer, had won eleven regional and national competitions. Vocalist Mallory had enough award certificates to wallpaper a bathroom. Writing awards, soccer and field hockey medals and academic awards marked the successes of Kyle.

Mrs. Daley leaned in to peer especially close at the Pitt awards bearing Reece's name. The Pitt, named after a turn-of-the-century Prescott graduate, was a gold medallion roughly the size of a half dollar. The Pitt was awarded to students who managed a year of perfect attendance. The three awards Reece had earned sat in a neat row, each on a bed of navy velvet in its own gold leather box.

Bailey had two Pitts and Kelsey had one.

Christopher had never earned a Pitt.

The argument between the two fathers was fast climbing to an ungodly volume, so Mrs. Daley, her eyes tearing, focused her attention on the portrait of the six Wyndham children.

The three older girls stood behind the three younger ones. The girls were various shades of brunette, from dark, sunlit honey to sable and jet. Three of the girls had dark brown eyes, two had amber and one had hazel. Each girl had Sara Wyndham's fine, perfect eyebrows and striking cheekbones. Two of the girls had Craig Wyndham's dimples.

The Wyndham daughters were six of the prettiest girls Mrs. Daley had ever seen, and as the head of Nicole Payton Modeling, Inc., she encountered plenty of pretty.

"My sisters have your book," announced a sleep-raspy voice at Mrs. Daley's side.

She turned to see one of the Wyndham girls, probably the youngest. Her long hair was the color of bittersweet chocolate and fell past the shoulders of her lavender nightgown. She couldn't have been older than twelve, possibly thirteen.

Mrs. Daley wiped her eyes with her hand and cleared her throat. "Which sisters?" she asked.

"Reece and Bailey." The young girl rubbed her eyes and yawned. "They got them at school last week."

Mrs. Daley had given a health and beauty seminar to Prescott's senior and junior girls, and each student and faculty member had received a complimentary copy of her latest book, *The Best in You.* The Prescott visit had been a carefully orchestrated part of the publicity campaign to kick off her book tour.

"Which one of these girls is Reece?" Mrs. Daley asked.

Instead of pointing to one of the subjects in the studio portrait above the sofa, the sleepy-eyed girl took a gilded frame from an end table. She handed it to Mrs. Daley.

In the photo, a long-legged girl in a navy and gold Prescott Track uniform smiled modestly from the top step of an awards podium. She proudly displayed a gold medal hanging around her neck. Reece's hair was short in the photo, long in the portrait. Mrs. Daley preferred the shorter do. Reece's long hair had been gorgeous, but the shorter style better complemented her face, giving her a wholesome, pixyish sort of beauty.

"Who's my dad fighting with?"

Before Mrs. Daley could answer, the noise of the argument reached a crescendo.

"Put yourself in my position!" Mr. Daley yelled, and his wife had no trouble picturing the large, snake-like vein that was undoubtedly pulsing in the center of his forehead. "My son is abducted, from my home, without a trace. The abductor had to possess intimate knowledge of both my household and my son's habits. Only today have I learned of this mystery girlfriend who happens to be your daughter. How do I know that your daughter was really abducted? How can I be sure that you aren't the mastermind behind my son's kidnapping? People have done worse to make a quick dime."

A deadly silence followed Mr. Daley's tirade and Mrs. Daley took that moment to intervene. "Cool it, Augie," she said, entering the kitchen. "Reece Wyndham is in the same danger as

Christopher, perhaps more. The Wyndhams have nothing to do with the kidnapping, and Reece isn't Christopher's girlfriend."

"How can you possibly know that?" Mr. Daley ranted. "You'd never heard of the girl before today."

"A girl like Reece wouldn't have our son on a silver platter."

Mrs. Daley's calm along with Mrs. Wyndham's coffee soothed their husbands' ruffled feathers.

"What should we do when they contact us?" Mrs. Wyndham pulled her bathrobe closer about her trim frame.

"We give them what they want," Mr. Daley said.

"We have to notify the authorities," Mr. Wyndham insisted. "I have a friend on the St. Louis City police force. He'll keep it quiet."

"You don't understand the gravity of this situation," Mr. Daley started, his voice rising once again. "There is absolutely no way to prevent leaks, especially when the Daley name is involved. Do you have any idea what might happen to our children if the media gets wind of this? Silence is the only way to contain this."

"Here we go again," Mr. Wyndham grimaced, gripping the wheels of his chair so hard the dark-brown skin of his knuckles paled.

The kitchen door swung open, and Mrs. Daley's early morning information officer entered.

"Kyle, sweetheart." Mrs. Wyndham forced cheer into her voice as she bustled her daughter toward the door. "Go back to bed, honey. It's too early to be up."

Mr. Daley reached into the inner breast pocket of his jacket and retrieved a cellular phone scarcely bigger than a credit card. "Here." He angrily shoved it at Mr. Wyndham. "If you insist on dragging the police into this, go ahead. Just don't tie up your home line. I don't intend to miss the next contact."

"I've had as much of you as I can stand for one night, Daley," Mr. Wyndham growled. "I'm not going to just sit here and do nothing, while—"

Kyle shrugged off her mother's hands. "Daddy?" She crossed one bare foot over the other. Her tiny toes were painted a pearly shade of pink.

"Craig, maybe we should wait before calling the station," Mrs. Wyndham said. "Let's think about this, just for a minute."

Mr. Wyndham turned on his wife. "Now you're giving me orders, Sara?"

"Mom?" Kyle said, a quiver in her voice.

"Please, go back to bed, love," Mrs. Wyndham told her.

"But there's—"

"Damn it, Kyle, go upstairs and go to bed!" Mr. Wyndham yelled.

Kyle burst into tears. Her father had never once shouted at her in her entire life. Mrs. Wyndham gathered her into an embrace and soothed her with kisses.

"I got scared," Kyle sobbed. "There was a man outside. All the yelling woke me up, and I was looking out of my window and I saw him. He was wearing a long coat."

Mrs. Wyndham consoled Kyle while Mr. Wyndham and Mr. Daley rushed to the front door. Mr. Wyndham threw it open. The blue-grey light of dawn framed him as he stared down at the front step. He leaned out of his chair and picked up a CD centered on the plastic welcome mat. The CD case had no markings. He swallowed hard. Glanced over his shoulder at Mr. Daley, he said, "We've been contacted."

"What the hell is this, a joke?"

Mr. Daley's irate question broke the tense silence that had ensued in their wait for something other than black screen to appear on the television in the living room console. The disc had been running for a few seconds that felt like forever.

"Just shut up," Mr. Wyndham snapped.

The two men would have begun fighting again if Mrs. Daley hadn't gasped and clutched the pearls at her throat.

Christopher's scratched and bruised face filled the television screen, the image wavering. He bowed his head to read from a piece of paper. "One," came his deep, clear voice, "do not involve the police, the FBI or any other investigative authorities. Two, carry out each directive as it is received. Any deviation will result in my death. Three, I will be returned, alive and unharmed, upon the receipt of ten million dollars in Swiss bearer bonds. You have until the close of business Tuesday to acquire the funds necessary to secure my release. Four, you will be contacted at noon on Tuesday and given instructions for the exchange of the bonds for me. Any deviation or outside interference will result in my death."

An anguished sob tore from Mrs. Wyndham. "What about Reece?" she whispered. Mrs. Daley firmly clasped her hand, but the question went unanswered as a filmy plastic grocery bag suddenly swooped down to enclose Christopher's head. A scream beyond Christopher matched the one in the Wyndham living room. Mrs. Daley fell to her knees before the television, banging a fist on the screen as Christopher thrashed violently, struggling for breath against the plastic molded to his face.

The image on screen dizzily bobbed and weaved with the movement of the person holding the camera. The camera pulled back, showing a massive, hooded figure pinning Christopher's arms to his chair. A smaller hooded man tightly cinched the bag at his throat.

Christopher bucked and twisted against the chair, but the men held him tight.

"Oh, God, help him," Mrs. Wyndham pleaded woefully.

God seemed to respond. A sound like that of a rubber mallet striking a large ham snapped off screen, and the big man holding Christopher fell away with a grunt. His arms free, Christopher clawed through the bag. His coughing and gasping almost drowned out the fracas going on in the blurry background.

"Turn it off, you idiot!" the smaller figure yelled, but not before a long, denim-clad leg swung in a wide arc and caught him in the jaw with an expertly executed crescent kick.

The camera crazily followed the movements of Christopher and his hooded captors as they rushed toward the person who had delivered that kick. The picture was helplessly out of focus but the audio was clear.

"Stop her!"

"That li'l bitch sucker-punched me!"

"Shoot her!"

"I cain't turn it off!"

The camera abruptly dropped, providing a clear shot of a splintered wood floor. A loud pop, like the sound of a squirrel tripping a bare spot in a live wire, chilled the blood of the parents in the cozy Wyndham living room.

The audio died and the screen went black.

She drew her knees closer, making herself as small as possible in a corner of the darkened room. Her eyes tightly closed, she hoped she was too small for Oliver and his cousins to notice when they returned, but the insides of her eyelids became miniature screens replaying the scenes of her death.

They had killed her.

Just as surely as Oliver had tried to smother Christopher, Oliver had killed her when she attempted to stop him.

Christopher had read the list of demands and then Oliver had muttered something about making a point.

Reece's body had gone into action before her brain could consider the consequences. She had dealt a one-two punch combination to Ross's kidneys, knocking him away from Christopher. She followed that with a crescent kick to Oliver's face. While Gentry fumbled with the camera on Oliver's phone, she had dashed for the door. Ross had intercepted her. Oliver, the killer, had aimed a black object at her and fired.

A phantom pain almost as excruciating as the real thing had been jolted through her. Silver fireworks had burst under her skin after the shot. Big, blotchy misshapen stars had lurched across her field of vision as her body skipped directly into rigor mortis, locking her breath in her chest and plunging her into a darkness more complete than that of their prison.

She took deep, shaky breaths that reminded her lungs of their responsibility to the rest of her body. With each inhalation, she smelled ozone, singed fabric and her own burnt flesh, the perfume of her death.

Christopher had rescued her from the blackness. He had begged- no, a Daley would never beg. He had *demanded* that she come back. And she had, but not without his help. He had been counting robotically and compressing her chest when a sputter of stale air, air that he had forced into her, erupted from her.

As soon as she could sit up and move, she had done so, putting herself as far from him as possible.

"You weren't sick," she accused, choking on the air he had given her. "Mr. Huxhold asked me to bring the review sheets to you because he thought you were out sick." A coughing spasm seized her. "But you weren't sick at all."

"What are you talking about?" His voice as shaky as his hands. He reached for her.

She had swatted him away, wincing from the pain of the burns in her chest.

"I wouldn't be here if you had gone to school!" she had screamed, not caring if Thing One, Thing Two and the Cat in the Hood heard her.

Christopher sat against the opposite wall, watching the rise and fall of her shoulders in the dim light afforded by the louvers in the bathroom. He was afraid to look away, afraid she would stop breathing again.

He hadn't seen what started the fight. He had only just identified the object in Oliver's hand, a Pulse One taser gun most likely stolen from the security office at the Janus, when Oliver used it to shoot Reece.

The Pulse One could deliver up to 50,000 volts and when the electrical probes hit her, Reece more than fell. She had been thrown to the floor, the probes sticking just below her left collarbone. She had stiffened, then bucked violently just once before she seemed to melt into the dirty floorboards. Only the whites of her eyes showed before her eyelids slowly closed, pushing a lone tear toward her right temple.

Oliver and his damned cousins had just stood and watched her turn a sickening shade of purple. Oliver had snatched the probes from Reece's clothing while Ross took the chair they had brought. The cousins followed Oliver from the room, locking the door behind them and turning off the light. Christopher had rushed to Reece and mined her neck for a pulse, but had felt nothing.

He shuddered at the memory.

Ever since he had revived her, she had sat in the corner, curled into a tiny ball, as night crept into day.

I should go to her, he thought. *But she doesn't want me. I can't blame her.*

He passed a hand through his hair and thumped his head against the wall, all the while keeping his eyes on her. Ten million dollars. It was laughable that someone actually thought he was worth that much. For the Daleys, the sum really wasn't that much at all. Demanding $10 million from Augie Daley was like demanding a cow from Iowa.

He ran the fingertips of his right hand over the bare spot on his left wrist where his TAGHeuer sports watch had been. Ross Ligget now wore that watch.

He closed his eyes to shut out the sight of the splintering floor, the peeling wallpaper, the patches of mold it revealed, and the thick boards nailed across the window. There was a light fixture in the ceiling, a dual socket with two bare bulbs, but the wall switch was outside the room. The air vent in the bathroom allowed the very slightest breeze, which came into their cell accompanied by the faint aromas of diesel fuel, ripe corn and mildew. The light filtering through the air vent was quickly fading. The decrepit room was a study in early morning shadows and grays. The one spot of color was the glossy chocolate of Reece's bowed head.

Whether she pushed him away again, for now he was all she had, so he went to her. He cradled her in the curve of his chest and left arm. He had no experience consoling anyone, so he doubted he did the right thing by burying his fingers in her hair and pressing her head to his shoulder.

He murmured what he hoped were words of comfort, quieting only when she began to weep. Ragged sobs wet his T-shirt as she drew her knees between them and twined an arm around his neck. He held her until her tears stopped and her trembling ceased. He embraced her until she fell into a tense and twitchy sleep.

His head rested against hers, his quiet breathing caressing the curve of her ear. His right hand moved along her back, his fingers tracing her spine through her sweater. When his hand kept going, sweeping softly over her hip and along the length of her outer thigh, she opened her eyes.

She pulled her arm from his waist, untangled her fingers from the silky hair at his nape, and clumsily got to her feet. As much as she needed to stretch her rigid muscles and empty her bladder, she wanted even more to crawl back into his embrace and sleep until their nightmare was over.

He rubbed his eyes and yawned. The room was warm but he shivered without her heat beside him.

"I didn't go to your house because of the review sheet," she admitted quietly. "I wanted to ask you to go to Logan's party with me. That's the real reason I volunteered to bring the sheet to you. I apologize for yelling at you."

His ink-blue eyes, painfully lovely in the shadowy gloom of their prison, fixed on her. His eyes were framed by girlishly long lashes, which were the same jet hue as the tousled waves of hair on his head.

"I'm sorry I pushed you away." She clenched her hands into fists to stop them from shaking. "I'm sorry I blamed you. I know this isn't your fault."

"You were half right," he said. "I wasn't sick, but I didn't skip school yesterday. I only missed Mr. Huxhold's class. I skipped so I could pick up U2 tickets."

"You like U2?"

"Not particularly."

"U2 is my favorite band." She brushed away the moisture dotting her lower lashes.

"I know. I heard you and Evan Hamilton talking in the lounge about the concert."

Her eyes were large and dark and liquid as she looked at him. He couldn't form his next thought until she lowered her gaze. "I was going to call you Saturday morning, to ask you to go with me."

"Today's Saturday. Ask me now and save yourself a roaming charge."

"Reece, would you go to the concert with me tomorrow night?"

"Sure." Her voice cracked, and she bit her lower lip to stave off more tears.

"I'll pick you up at six. We can have dinner at La Giaconda's before the show."

"I'd like that." A faint smile softened her worried expression. "Chris?"

"Christopher."

"Why can't your dad get the money today? Most banks are open at least until noon."

He dreaded telling her that banking hours didn't apply to Augie Daley. With a mere phone call his father could gain access to funds all over the world at any time of day or night.

"It doesn't matter when the banks open," he said, holding her troubled gaze. "Oliver wants to make the transfer on Tuesday. I think...I think he wants to keep us here for so long just to show that he can."

Chapter Four

Mr. Daley stood on the Wyndham's rear deck, speaking quietly into the wireless phone he white-knuckled at his ear. Three tousle-haired teenagers crowded into the second floor bathroom window to get a look at the top of his head.

"Who is he?" Bailey whispered.

"He doesn't look like any of dad's friends." Kelsey elbowed her younger sister, Mallory, to make more room for herself.

Mallory climbed onto the lid of the toilet and parted the lace curtains a bit more to get a better look. "He looks like that lawyer on channel 30 who does those 'Just Leave It to Me and Cash You'll See' commercials."

Kyle staggered into the bathroom, her right cheek imprinted with the pattern of her rumpled bed sheets. "He's here because of Reece," she volunteered somberly. "I have to pee."

The three older Wyndham girls left Kyle to take care of her business in private. They went into the cluttered room shared by Reece and Bailey to continue their hushed speculations.

"Reece didn't come home last night," Bailey said. She had awakened to see her sister's empty bunk. Taryn's twin bed was empty, too, because she now resided with her husband in Clayton, Brentwood's posh neighbor.

"Wow." Mallory, her earthy brown eyes wide, sat cross-legged on her bunk bed. "I'll bet Dad is ready to split a biscuit!"

"Maybe that guy on the patio is a sports agent," Kelsey offered. She merrily flapped the sleeves of her flannel nightshirt as she bounced on Taryn's bed. "Maybe Reece is gonna do commercials for Nike or Gatorade."

"He's probably another scout from some college who needs her legs," Bailey suggested. "He dresses a lot better than the other ones who've come here."

"Let's go downstairs!" Kelsey vaulted over a stack of hairstyling and celebrity infotainment magazines, but Bailey grabbed the tail of her nightshirt and reeled her back.

"We should wait," Mallory said. "Dad hates it when he thinks we're spying."

"Mom and Dad will think there's something wrong if we *don't* go downstairs," Kelsey said, her amber eyes twinkling. "They know we're up. They probably heard your big feet hit the floor when you got out of bed."

"Your feet are the same size as mine," Mallory said.

"That reminds me. Can I wear your new sneaks to the dance studio today?"

"Of course not," Mallory scoffed. "Those shoes cost me three weeks of babysitting money and I've only worn them twice."

"You're so selfish," Kelsey snapped.

"You're so ugly," Mallory countered.

"I look just like you." Kelsey smiled sweetly. "Everyone says so."

"Reece is in trouble." Kyle stood in the doorway, the toes of her right foot covering those of her left. She was wearing the shark's tooth ankle bracelet Reece had given her for her last birthday. "Reece and Christopher Daley are in trouble."

The Daleys stood facing each other on the Wyndhams' patio, Mr. Daley clutching his wife's hands to his heart. "I should have sent him to school on the East Coast or in England," he whispered fervently. "He would have been far from here, well out of harm's way!" Mrs. Daley embraced him, her body rigid with fear. "They want to keep him, to torment me," Mr. Daley muttered into her softly scented shoulder. "They want to make me suffer!"

Mrs. Daley cupped his face, and her tear-swollen eyes burned into his. "You really do love him, don't you?"

He tore her arms away. "What kind of question is that?" he hissed, his voice breaking.

Mrs. Daley blinked away fresh tears. She wasn't the first Mrs. Daley, or even the second. She was the third Mrs. Christopher Daley II and until now, her biggest fear had been that she wouldn't be the last.

Despite his two previous marriages, Augie Daley's only

child and sole heir was Christopher. He had always treated his son accordingly, carefully grooming him for life in the public eye and to someday assume the helm of one of the world's largest business conglomerates.

Not once had the third Mrs. Daley ever heard her husband say, "I love you," to their son, who often fell short of Mr. Daley's high expectations. She couldn't remember the last time Augie had said "I love you" to her, and she desperately wanted to hear those words. She would trade every penny of their combined fortunes if Augie would look upon her with the same adoration that Craig and Sara Wyndham bestowed upon one another, especially at a time like this.

Mr. Daley grabbed his wife by her upper arms. "I love Christopher," he insisted, his pale emerald eyes searching the ocean blue-green of hers. "I love both of you more than anything on this earth. With everything I am and everything I have. I can't get my son back until those cretins tell me that I can. I love him, Nicole. I'd give my own life for one more chance to tell him that."

"Maybe we should do as Craig wants," Mrs. Daley suggested through her tears. "The police could help—"

"No," Mr. Daley said sharply, cutting her off. "Absolutely not. They will kill him. That CD is proof."

She bowed her head to his chest. "Augie, what can we do?"

"The only thing we can. We have to wait."

Christopher's stomach growled.

Reece giggled.

Her laughter was surprisingly comforting. "That's my pet wombat," he said.

"Starving us must be part of their plan."

"I wouldn't put it past Leighton Oliver. He's one of my father's vice-presidents. He always stares at me and he's always too friendly. I saw a memo he wrote once, totally ratting out one of the other veep's for taking a sick day. He found out that she was using her sick time to work on a book project. He's a total bastard."

He sat on the floor, facing Reece in the dark. As the day had worn on and the sun moved to the other side of the house, the scant light had grown dimmer until it vanished.

"Do you think your dad will figure out that Leighton Oliver is behind this?" Reece asked.

"I don't know. My father doesn't speak to me about the people who work for him. He only lectures about the work itself. He's practically already got a corner office reserved for me at the Janus."

"You don't want to be a corporate raider when you grow up?" she teased.

"I'm not expected to be anything else. Even my mom expects me to take over D.I.I. someday. When I was little, she used to tell me that I could be anything I wanted."

"Your mother seems really nice. She's so pretty."

"Have you read her book?"

"No, not yet. I've, uh, had too much homework." She would have preferred vomiting on him again to confessing that her copy of *The Best in You* was currently propping up the shorter third leg of her bedroom dresser.

"It's three hundred glossy, vanilla-scented pages of pigeon poop and you know it," he said.

"The idea behind it is pretty cool. That women improve with age."

"Mom wrote that because she's old. She'll be forty-five in November but she tells everyone she's thirty-six."

"She looks twenty-five, so she must be doing something right." Her fingers absently went to the scorched spots on her sweater, and Christopher felt a sharp surge of guilt. "My mom is forty and everybody thinks she's my older sister."

Christopher often saw Mrs. Wyndham running laps on Prescott's outdoor track after school. A lot of guys found reasons to stray past the track when Mrs. Wyndham was out there. She was the most attractive teacher at Prescott, maybe even prettier than his own mother, simply because she was so down-to-earth.

"My mom says that women get better as they get older," Reece said confidently. "My best years are ahead of me." *If I live to see them,* she added to herself.

"Too bad I'm not a woman. I think I peaked two years ago."

"You're really not as rotten as you want people to think. Why do you act like such a snobby knob at school?"

" 'Snobby knob,'" he repeated thoughtfully. "What a quaint little term."

"You're doing it now. Being a snobby knob."

"Sorry. Force of habit."

"Why do you act that way? It puts people off when you treat them with contempt and condescension."

"You mean when I act like a snob."

"You said it, not me."

"Do you know what it's like to have people pretend to be your friend just so your father will give their father a job, or donate money to their organization, or so you'll have a party at your house and invite a hundred of *their* closest friends? No one likes me, Reece. No one ever has. People like the Daley fortune, not me. I'm not a person. I'm a thing. Christopher August Daley Number Three. It's a label, not a name. Forgive me if I have an attitude about it."

"I wouldn't have come to your house to ask you out if I didn't genuinely like *you,*" she said. "I don't give two squirts of squid ink about your money."

"Sure," he said skeptically. "Whatever you say. Everyone thinks they're above it until they get close to it."

"Courtney Miller says you haven't dated anyone in two years. Why did you want to ask me to the U2 concert? Because you thought I was a money-grubber? I can't wait until we get out of this and we can go back to ignoring each other."

He stood up and paced in a small circle. "I never ignored you. I couldn't have ignored you even if I wanted to."

"Oh, really? I say hello to you, sit next to you in class, ask you for American Literature notes that I already had. You barely ever looked at me. What else did I have to do to get your attention, throw myself in your lap?"

"It would have been more direct."

"I hate you."

"That's too bad, because I really like you."

She made a noise, something between a snort and a laugh. "Since when?"

"Since our sophomore carnival."

"That was two years ago," she scoffed.

He dropped beside her. His voice was very near her ear. "You were in the dunking booth, dressed as a mermaid. Your hair was long then, and pinned up with ribbons and flowers woven through it. The flowers were daisies, I think. You sat up there on the bench, flipping that fake tail. You splashed water on Mr. Edwards and totally drenched him. He thought it was an accident, but if he had turned around and seen your smile, you'd have been in study detention until graduation."

Joy washed over her as she recalled that sunlit day of silliness and laughter. "Felix Nayland was the first one to dunk me," she recalled. "He did it on the first try. Who knew he had such a good arm? The water ruined my hair and makeup, but it was fun."

"You looked like a wet cat."

"You really know how to ruin a mood."

"I wasn't aware that I was creating one."

"They were daisies."

"Where would a mermaid find daisies?"

"I like daisies so I used daisies. Daisies are my favorite flower. They're so ordinary. They aren't too delicate, like tulips, or pretentious and intimidating, like roses. They aren't glamorous, either, but they catch your attention with their simple beauty."

Just like you, he thought.

"If you've liked me since the tenth grade, why didn't you ever say so?" she asked. "Or even say hello to me once in a while?"

He blindly made his way to the window. He pulled at the end of a plank nailed over it. "I'm not one for standing in line."

"What do you mean?"

"There's always at least five guys waiting to ask you out, each of them a lot less snobby and a lot more knobby than I am. I don't date much, for obvious reasons."

"They aren't obvious to me."

"Come on, Reece," he snapped. "I know what they call me at school. Christopher Snobbins is my favorite. Christopher Gayley is a bit unfair, though."

"Gayley?" she echoed. "I've never heard that one."

"Larry Odenkirk thinks I'm gay."

"Larry Odenkirk is a rancid goat turd. Why does he think you're gay?"

"Because I don't date much. Because I don't date at all."

"Well...are you gay? I mean, gay guys really like me. This one time at an invitational track meet, this gay cheerleader told me that I was the only girl he ever had heterosexual feelings for. It was right after I got all my hair cut off, so maybe—"

"I like girls, Reece. They just don't like *me*. They like my BMW and the restaurants I take them to, they like my father's helicopter and his vacation houses and—"

"I don't care about those things and I don't care about your money."

"Ha! You'd make a terrible rich person, Reece. Rich people never say, 'I don't care about money.' They don't talk about money at all. It would be like talking about air or sunlight."

"Have I ever given you the impression that I want anything from you other than the chance to get to know you better? We don't need money for that. If this room and those awful men are what having money gets you, then I hope I never have any."

"Why did you want me to go to Logan's party with you?" he asked, a bitter edge to his voice.

She stood. Her knees threatened to give, but thankfully they supported her. "On the first day of school, when Logan came into the dining hall, I thought he was the most gorgeous creature on this planet. As cute and nice as Logan is, *you're* the one I can't stop thinking about. You're cold and unpleasant, but for some idiotic reason, when I look at you, I can't catch my breath. You're so damn handsome. You've got your mom's model mouth and your dad's superhero jaw. And sometimes, I can't even remember my own name when I look at you. It has nothing to do with your stupid car, or your stupid house, or your stupid, stupid name. It's because of your stupid eyes and your stupid smile. I can't believe I was stupid enough to tell you this." She picked her way to the bathroom, and closed the creaky door behind her.

Chapter Five

"Thanks for hiding my backpack," she said, bringing the canvas and nylon bag with her when she left the bathroom.

"I didn't want them to take any of your things. Once they got us here, I guess they forgot about it."

He had stuffed the heavy bag into the rusting, claw-footed bathtub. The tub had been turned on its side, its top facing the wall, making a perfect hiding place.

Reece sat on the floor, opened her bag, and withdrew two granola bars. She offered one to Christopher.

"I hate granola." He ripped open the green foil packaging and ate half of the cinnamon-flavored bar in one chomp.

"It's good for you." She gulped hers down in very unladylike bites.

"That's why I hate it."

She went through her bag, giving it a cursory inventory though she couldn't see a thing. "Everything seems to be here."

"Do you have anything we can use to escape?"

"Sure, if we can make a bomb with my lab timer, two tampons, and a mini tube of tartar control toothpaste."

"Could I see your timer?" He felt around in the dark until he caught her wrist, and then he plucked the timer from her hand and took it into the bathroom. He stood on the side of the tub and angled the timer at the louvers of the air vent until he captured enough light to read the digital numbers.

"It's one o'clock," he said, returning it to her. "We've been missing for almost twenty-four hours."

The lights came on, drowning them in a tide of brightness. A cold bomb of adrenaline exploded in Reece's stomach. Her flight or fight response settled on the latter, since she had no place to run. Christopher, his eyes stinging, stood between her and whatever threat the light would bring.

Ross and Gentry entered the room, the cloyingly sweet aroma of wet chewing tobacco and damp earth clinging to them.

Ross sauntered into the center of the room with his thumbs hooked through the belt loop of his dungarees.

Gentry stayed near the door. Carrying a domed tray, his fingernails black crescents against the gleaming silver, he was a caricature of backwoods hospitality.

Ross shrugged a meaty shoulder bared by the strappy T-shirt pulled over his hulking frame. "Y'all hungry?" His rumbling bass started Reece's knees knocking. If a grizzly bear could talk, she imagined it would sound like Ross.

"Y'all gotta be hungry," Ross said knowingly. He nodded at Gentry, who set the tray on the floor and used his foot to shoot it toward Christopher.

"Go on." With a hard kick to Christopher's calf, Ross encouraged him to take the tray.

Christopher retrieved the dish and brought it to Reece. He lifted the dome carefully.

She closed her eyes. She had seen an old black and white film once, *Whatever Happened to Baby Jane?* If Baby Jane's Rodent á là King was on the platter, Reece was sure that she would upchuck all over the place.

"That shor' look good, don't it?" Gentry beamed. "I bet you eat fancy like that all the time, don'tcha?"

Reece opened her eyes to see ten colossal prawns hooked over a glass bowl filled with cocktail sauce. The bowl rested on a sparkling bed of ice.

"Go on, eat up," Ross said. "Lester brought that special for you, all the way from St. Louis."

"I can't eat this." Christopher's stomach growled in protest.

Ross stomped over to the dish and grabbed the tail of a prawn. Reece shrank away from him. "We ain't gon' poison you. Not yet, leastways." He shoved the succulent pink meat into his mouth and noisily devoured it.

"I'm allergic to shellfish," Christopher said. "Leighton Oliver knows that."

A surprised grunt found its way past the chewed prawn in Ross's mouth. "Ain't that too bad," he laughed. "Lester shor' pulled a good one on you!" He took the tray, laughing, and shoved another prawn into his mouth.

"Who is Lester?" Christopher asked.

"Our cousin," Gentry offered eagerly. "He changed his first name to Leighton when he finished up at Juniper Falls High. Soon as he got his scholarship up to Winterhill College, he started puttin' on all kinds 'a airs. He cut his hair 'n started wearin' fancy clothes. He didn't hardly never come home no more, 'n when he did, he always had some story 'bout all the pretty girls 'n smart people he was friendly with. Wasn't nobody fooled, jus' 'cause he changed his name. His daddy was one 'a them mean-tempered Olivers, but his mama was a Liggett, same as our daddy."

"Leighton Oliver used to be Lester Oliver," Christopher smirked.

"Yup," Gentry chuckled. "He wanted a fancy name for college. Said he didn't want nobody to know he was Ozark trash an'—"

"Shut up, Gentry." Ross's order closed Gentry's mouth as quickly and efficiently as flipping a switch.

Ross turned his squinty eyes on Reece. "You real hungry, ain't you girl?"

Reece had no appetite at all.

Ross moved closer to her, his eyes glinting. "You let 'ol Ross know when you get hungry enough, li'l lady. I got somethin' special to fill you up."

"Pig."

Whatever designs Ross had on Reece went on hold. He turned to Christopher.

Christopher pulled himself to his full height. At five feet and ten inches, he was still significantly shorter than Ross, who probably outweighed him by at least eighty pounds.

"Ross," Gentry whimpered, nervously shifting from foot to foot. "Lester said to leave 'im be. Lester said not to let 'im *revoke* you."

"Oh, ah'm gon' leave 'im be," Ross said docilely, his breath reeking of seafood and wet tobacco. With a quickness surprising for a creature of his size, he grabbed Christopher by his shoulders and spun him, slamming his chest into the wall. He delivered two crushing blows to the small of Christopher's back, and Christopher slid along the wall to the floor, clutching at his back and cringing in pain.

"It's like shootin' fish in a barrel." Ross grinned merrily, shaking out his fist.

"Ain't no fun in that," Gentry mumbled.

"The fun is watchin' 'em die," Ross said. He and Gentry left, slamming the door and locking it behind them. The light went off , plunging Christopher and Reece in darkness. Reece crawled to him, but he shrugged her off when she tried to help him sit up.

"Can't you see that they're just looking for reasons to hurt you?" she whispered.

"Do you have anything else to eat in that suitcase you call a backpack?" he grimaced. "I'm fine."

She felt around with her hands until she located her bag. "How did Lester know you were allergic to shellfish?"

"I don't know. Maybe he read it in a gossip column, or saw me skip the seafood appetizer at one of my father's philanthropic events. Ol' Lester did his homework."

"I have a banana, a Granny Smith apple, a roll of Lifesavers, three pieces of sugarless gum, three granola bars, a protein bar, five oatmeal cookies, and a bottle of spring water. It's only half full."

"Pig."

"Didn't that word just get you into a world of hurt? I'm not a pig, I have a high metabolism," she said defensively. "If I didn't eat all the time, I'd look like Olive Oyl."

"You are a little two-dimensional up top."

"My mom says that with legs like mine, I don't need boobs to catch a guy's eye."

"Your mom's right. So what's on the menu tonight, Emeril?"

Reece chose the apple, the banana, two oatmeal cookies and the Lifesavers. She peeled the banana and gave Christopher half.

"This is the best banana I've ever had," he said, gulping it down. "If I ever eat another banana, there's no way it could taste as good as this one."

"I've never been so hungry." She took a bite of the juicy apple, and the tart sweetness of the firm flesh sparked her salivary glands. She passed the apple to Christopher.

A quarter of it disappeared in one noisy bite. He had to consciously restrain himself from devouring the whole thing. "When we get out of this, I'm taking you to the Carnegie Deli. They make the best club sandwiches."

"We could go there instead of La Giaconda's, before the concert."

"The Carnegie Deli is in New York City. We'd have to make a weekend of it."

"I've never been to New York City."

"Then it's time you went. It would be fun to take you jogging in Central Park."

"You like to run?"

"Sometimes. I like to jog in Central Park because there's so much to see. I like to run at the beach sometimes, too."

"I love to run." The edge smoothed off her hunger, she could devote her thoughts to her one great passion. "When I run, I always reach a point where I feel like I could just go on forever. When we lived in Maryland, we used to go to Ocean City every summer. One of the things I've always wanted to do was take off my clothes and just run along the beach until there was no more beach to run on. It would be so wonderful to feel the sun on my skin, the wind in my hair and the sand between my toes. Doesn't it sound incredible? Can't you just picture it?"

"Yes," he said thickly, in answer to both questions. He pictured it so vividly, he completely forgot about his aching back, the darkness and his hunger.

"Pass the apple, please."

He squinted, as if sunlight glinting off the ocean was in his eyes.

"Christopher?"

Like a rubber band stretched almost to its breaking point, his attention snapped back to their prison. "Huh?" he said stupidly.

"I asked you to pass the apple. You're gobbling it all up."

"You sure know how to ruin a mood," he said, seeing only darkness as he handed her the apple.

Chapter Six

Craig Wyndham sat at the head of the dining table as he had every other Sunday morning. His gaze lit on his wife and each of his precious daughters. Reece's absence sent an arrow of pain through his heart and he inwardly cursed his helplessness.

"You okay, Dad?" Taryn Wyndham Barton asked. She sat to his right, her dark eyes bright with concern. "You look like you're coming down with something."

Mrs. Wyndham clutched her husband's hand.

"This is about Reece, isn't it, Daddy?" Bailey asked pensively.

A furrow appeared between Kelsey's eyes. "That man who was here yesterday morning, I've seen him before. He's on television, right?"

"Something's really wrong, I just know it," Mallory fretted. She glanced at her mother, a plea in her eyes for everything to be all right. "Reece isn't at a friend's house, is she? You don't know where she is, do you? Is that why you asked me and Bailey all those questions about what we did after school Friday? Why did you lie to us?"

Mrs. Wyndham patted her daughter's hand as she met her husband's gaze. *We can't keep lying to them,* her troubled gaze seemed to say.

"Girls," Mr. Wyndham began, "Christopher Daley was abducted from his home Friday afternoon. Somehow, Reece got involved."

"Augie Daley!" Kelsey launched out of her chair. "That's the guy who was on the deck yesterday morning."

"C. August Daley?" Taryn said, swallowing a lump of buttermilk pancake that had gone dry in her mouth. "He kidnapped Reece?"

"No, Taryn," Mrs. Wyndham said, addressing her first and fifth daughters in order, "Kelsey, take your seat and listen."

"Reece has been kidnapped?" Mallory's eyes filled with tears. "This is a joke, right?" She glanced timidly at her brother-in-law, Stirling Barton, who sat opposite her. "Is this some prank you and your friends at the television station put together? It isn't funny!"

"Yeah, Stirling," Kelsey said in an accusatory tone. She stood again, this time overturning her chair. "If this is some stupid joke of yours, my dad is gonna kick your—"

"Kelsey," Mr. Wyndham sighed tensely, "please sit down, and listen."

Kelsey righted her chair and plunked herself onto it, her objection to her father's request apparent in every muscle of her sixteen-year-old body. She narrowed her whiskey eyes at Stirling. *I'll* kick your ass, she mouthed at him.

Stirling stared at her, his heavy eyelids hooding his gaze, his full lips pulled into a smug grin. He was a sportscaster for KYNN, St. Louis' "Know Your News Network." He'd met Taryn a year ago, covering a martial arts competition in downtown St. Louis where Taryn had won the advanced women's division. He had asked her to dinner after the competition, and she had accepted. Nine months later, they married.

With her topaz eyes and copper-brown hair, Taryn had the face of an angel and the body of a video vixen. It hadn't been love at first sight for Stirling, but it was the closest he'd ever come to it. When Taryn brought him home to meet her family, he was hooked. Over and over and over again.

The Wyndham sisters, even Kyle, who had been only ten at the time, had been bridesmaids at the wedding. Stirling had felt like a sultan standing at the head of his own band of odalisques.

He almost laughed out loud at Kelsey's faith in her father's ability to kick someone's ass. To *kick* anything. Stirling sat taller and put his arm possessively over the back of Taryn's chair. Craig Wyndham's days of ruling the roost ended the second he became a human roller skate. As far as Stirling was concerned, he became man of the house, by extension, the day he married Taryn.

"When is Reece coming back?" Bailey asked. She shared a very special bond with Reece. They had been born in the same year, Reece in January and Bailey in December. They were each other's best friend and closest confidant.

"We don't know." Mrs. Wyndham's answer chilled everyone, with one exception.

Stirling got hot under his Tommy Hilfiger collar.

"Augie Daley isn't going to pay the ransom?" Stirling sputtered, his big biceps bunching within the tight sleeves of the black polo stretched across his chest and shoulders.

"Sara didn't say that," Mr. Wyndham stated firmly. "The kidnappers have asked for a very large sum, but the handoff can't be made until Tuesday."

"Oh, come on," Stirling said grandly, enjoying the sound of his own voice. "He expects us to believe that he can't wire the money from some offshore account and have it hand delivered within hours?"

"Look, Stirling," Mr. Wyndham said with dark warning. "Christopher was the target. Not Reece. We don't know how she got involved, but they don't want her."

Taryn shuddered and gripped Stirling's forearm.

"She's okay," Mrs. Wyndham forced herself to say, even though the scream they had heard at the end of the tape belied her words. Taryn was two months pregnant, and her parents had debated whether to tell her about the kidnapping at all.

"What makes you so sure she's okay?" Stirling left his chair to pace behind it. He was a big man and took up a lot of space as he moved about the small dining room. He had played professional football for three years before knee injuries permanently sidelined him.

"Reece and Christopher will be fine as long as we do what the kidnappers tell us to do," Mrs. Wyndham said. "We have to have faith in that."

"You're trusting them?" Stirling laughed. "They're kidnappers, not Sunday School teachers. Man, you guys are priceless!"

"Lay off, Stirling," Taryn warned. Her husband was much bigger than her, but Taryn would never let an opponent's size intimidate her. Especially if she was married to him.

"I will not 'lay off,'" he said, nonetheless taking his seat.

"What are the police doing? Why haven't I heard anything about this at KYNN?"

Mr. Wyndham slammed his fists on the table, sending half-empty plates and juice glasses jumping. He finally had Stirling's undivided attention. "The police are not to be notified," Mr. Wyndham growled between gritted teeth. "The media is not to be notified. The kidnappers will kill Christopher if we stray one hair from their agenda, and God only knows what they'll do to Reece. Do you understand me, Stirling? Is any of this getting through that block of granite you call a head?"

Kelsey stuck her tongue out at Stirling. Bailey and Mallory sobbed on their mother's shoulders. Kyle, her hazel eyes fixed on Stirling, shook her head in a sorrowful gesture that seemed ancient.

Stirling clenched his teeth so hard, his jaw cracked. He knew Mr. Wyndham didn't like him. The Wyndhams had practically begged Taryn to wait a couple of years before marrying him. That would have been fine with Stirling, but Taryn was an old-fashioned girl. She had absolutely refused to have sex with him before they were married. There was no way he was going to wait a couple of years to have her, so he had turned on the charm and convinced her to marry him against her family's wishes. She had been worth the wait, but he resolved to never again have the lower hand in any dealing with the Wyndham clan.

Taryn had wanted to settle in a spacious loft in University City. Stirling moved them to a small condo in Clayton. After the marriage, Taryn had wanted to keep her job as an electrical engineer with Eastern Missouri Public Utilities. Stirling made a few calls, doled out a few comps to Cardinals and Rams games, and he'd gotten his wife downsized. Taryn had wanted to wait a few years before having children. Stirling poked holes in her diaphragm.

Taryn had gotten things her way once, when she refused to have sex with him prior to marriage. No Wyndham would ever manipulate him into anything ever again.

"This will be resolved on Tuesday," Mr. Wyndham said.

"Until then, you have to behave normally. I know it won't be easy, but we can't afford to arouse suspicion. Reece and Christopher are depending on us. Can we do this for them?"

All around the table, heads slowly nodded, even the particularly large one centered above Stirling's shoulders.

"What are you going to wear?"

The rumbling of her stomach awakened Reece, and she sat up to find Christopher sitting in the dim, staring at her. She had no idea what he was talking about.

"It's Sunday morning. We have a date tonight," he explained. "What are you going to wear? Not jeans, I hope."

"What's wrong with my jeans?" She stood and stretched, then bent over her backpack. She withdrew a toothbrush and a tiny tube of toothpaste.

"Nothing, aside from the fact that you always wear jeans. I've never seen you in a dress or a skirt."

"I wear skirts on Dress-Up days."

"We're always traveling somewhere for the holidays, and we usually leave town a day or two early. I'm never around for Dress-Up days."

"And so we discover yet another drawback to skipping school," she said as she went into the bathroom.

She didn't know how her flippant remark affected him until she came out of the bathroom. The dim was just bright enough for her to see the wound she had inflicted gleaming in his eyes.

"I was kidding," she said. "I'm sorry I made that crack."

She dropped to her knees beside him. He shrugged away from her when she touched his shoulder. He took the toothbrush and toothpaste from her hand and went into the bathroom.

The mirror above the cracked and stained wall-mounted basin was broken. One small piece of the silver glass was still attached to the wall. It reflected the louvers of the air vent and narrow slices of a sky of clearest blue, a sky he hadn't seen since Friday afternoon.

He turned on both rusted faucets as far as they would go and got only a thin stream of cold water. He brushed his teeth, and cupping his hand beneath the water, he collected just enough to rinse his mouth. The water had a metallic taste and a sour smell so he spat it out quickly.

He knew that Reece hadn't meant to rub it in, the fact that she was in danger because of him. Ross's porcine face flashed before Christopher's eyes like a subliminal warning, and his stomach turned. They had hurt her twice already. If anything more happened to her, that too, would be his fault.

I can't let them hurt you again, he mutely promised. *I won't.*

She would have apologized again if he hadn't come out of the bathroom with a question for her already on his lips. "Do you go to church?" he asked.

She had assembled a feast on the back of her Spanish book: two oatmeal cookies, a Kit Kat, and two granola bars.

"We used to go every Sunday. We haven't been since my dad's accident."

"What religion are you?" He meant to eat slowly, to savor each precious bite of the soft, delicious oatmeal cookie that had surely come from the oven of Prescott Home Sciences teacher Sara Wyndham. He couldn't stop himself, and half of the palm-sized cookie disappeared into his mouth.

"Catholic." She nibbled her granola bar. Her last full meal had been lunch on Friday at Prescott. She had eaten four grilled cheese sandwiches, two bowls of tomato soup, three Rice Krispies treats, two glasses of milk and a handful of grapes. Ordinarily, she had the appetite of a team of lumberjacks, yet now she could barely stomach even a granola bar.

"Catholic," he repeated thoughtfully, snapping open the green foil wrapper of his granola bar. "Really."

"Yes, really," she said defensively.

"Do you go to confession?"

"Not anymore."

"Why not?" He gobbled the granola bar in two bites. "Wait,

don't tell me." He struck cinnamon-scented crumbs from his hands. "It's because you don't sin."

"I don't like it." She stared at her food. "And the word 'sin' is a noun to me, not a verb."

"Do you ever go to Mass?" He stared at her food.

"No. What is this, an Inquisition?"

"I'm just curious."

"What religion are *you*?" she countered testily.

"Episcopalian. Are you going to finish that?"

She gave her food to him. "Oh, you're the Henry-the-Eighth, Party-All-The-Time, runaway Catholics. You're against the Pope."

"I'm not against anyone."

"Do you believe in God?" She lowered her eyes as if she was ashamed of her own answer.

He stopped chewing. "I never thought about it."

"I believe in God. I believe in Hell, too, not one you go to after you die, but one you suffer through right here, while you're alive and can really feel it."

He stood on his knees and took her by the shoulders. "What brought this on? What's the matter?" He rolled his eyes toward the bare walls around them. "I mean, besides the obvious."

"There was a big fire at a housing development in St. Louis, when I was in the ninth grade. My dad is…*was*…a fireman. He was awesome. He loved his work so much. I loved going to the fire station and seeing him in his uniform. He looked like a superhero."

She paused to pick at one of the scorched marks on her sweater. "He was hurt. He carried three people out of that fire, and he was coming out with a fourth when burning debris fell on him. Three of his lumbar vertebrae were shattered. An inoperable bone fragment lodged in his spinal cord. My mother used to say that my dad is a man's man and a woman's fantasy. Now he can't walk. My big, strong, handsome daddy is in a wheelchair because God let him get hurt." She bowed her head and closed her eyes. If she was to be struck by lightening, she welcomed it with an unsettling calm. "God let Ross and Gentry Liggett get us. I believe in God but only because I'm scared not to. He'd probably do even worse to me if I didn't believe in Him."

"Do you really believe that God has it out for people like us? That's ridiculous. There are too many people and too many problems in the world for God to be worried about the Wyndhams or the Daleys. If anyone is made in His image, you Wyndhams are. You're all smart and beautiful and talented. Maybe God devotes his attention to the people who really need it, and leaves the care of people like us to ourselves. Or guardian angels, I don't know."

"You believe in guardian angels?"

"I wouldn't be alive if I didn't have one. I almost drowned off the coast of Cyprus when I was seven. I was bit by a snake in Egypt when I was eleven. I was thrown from a mustang on our ranch in Wyoming last year, and I landed smack on my head." He pushed his hair back to show her the scar where a fine row of sutures had closed his scalp. "And then there was the time my father's jet nearly crashed in the Grand Tetons."

"I almost ran in front of a car once," Reece said. "I was so into my run, I totally zoned out. Suddenly, it felt like someone grabbed me by the neck of my shirt and jerked me back onto the sidewalk. But there was nobody there when I turned around."

"You see? Your guardian angel was on his game."

"I guess it could have been worse, if my dad's guardian angel hadn't been at that fire," she considered. "My dad could have been killed. His guardian angel probably was there, begging him not to go back into that building. But my dad is so stubborn, he probably just didn't listen. He saved three people. He was their guardian angel."

"Guardian angels don't always come from Heaven." He brushed a stray lock of her hair from her forehead.

"You saved me yesterday," she said quietly. "I guess that makes you my angel."

Chapter Seven

Mr. Daley stood before a wall of bulletproof, mirrored glass, his hands clasped at the back of the five-thousand dollar suit he had worn to the fundraiser still in full swing on the tenth floor of the Janus.

The Daleys had relocated to the lavish penthouse at the top of the Janus, the fifty-story heart of Daley International, Inc. Daley Manor was contaminated, the air permeated by the presence of the men who had stolen Christopher, and Mrs. Daley had refused to stay there. Until Christopher's return, the Daleys would reside at the Janus.

The fundraiser, an event D.I.I. had sponsored annually for twenty-five years, raised scholarship money for student-athletes from Missouri high schools. Unbeknownst to Mr. Daley, who had nothing to do with the selection process, Taryn Wyndham had attended Washington University on a Daley Booster scholarship. Had he known, he might have marveled at how small the world could be.

Mr. Daley pressed his palm to the polarized, impact-resistant glass standing between him and the city. His son, his only child, was out there somewhere. Tears stung his eyes as he stared at the network of winding neighborhoods of the city and the hazy, tree-covered suburbs beyond. Nothing on the other side of the thick glass was beyond his grasp. Nothing except his son.

The world had never seemed so big.

"Taryn gave me a dress for my birthday. It's short and it has spaghetti straps. It's got tiny marguerite daisies on a wine-colored background. She got it in Mexico on her honeymoon."

Reece's soft voice soothed away the hard edge of the dark. Christopher could only guess that it was around the time he would have driven his sporty BMW into Brentwood to pick her up for their date. Despite the complete darkness, he kept his eyes closed, filling in the details of the dress as she described it.

"Red wine or white?"

"What?"

"The background of the dress. Red wine or white?"

"Red. You don't describe a dress as being white wine colored."

"Cabernet Sauvignon, Merlot, Bordeaux…which?"

"I don't know anything about wine, red or otherwise."

"My parents have allowed me to have wine with dinner since I was ten. My father is a collector. I guess I picked up the interest from him."

"My parents drink wine only on holidays. My dad only likes beer, but my mom likes to try new things. I had a white zinfandel wine cooler once, at a slumber party. I didn't really like it, but it was okay after I put a lot of ice cubes in it."

He laughed.

"I'm sorry I'm not a wine expert like you," she said, her self-consciousness edging her tone with spite. "You're not supposed to drink anyway. You're only eighteen."

"In France and Italy, just about everyone drinks wine. They don't do it irresponsibly like American teenagers do. They don't drink just to get drunk."

"What's the big deal about wine? Give me a cold glass of milk any day."

"I'll teach you how to appreciate wine when we go out for dinner."

"You won't get served," she said taunted merrily. "We're not in France or Italy."

"Then I'll take you to The Rise instead of La Giaconda. My father owns the place and the mâitre'd knows me. He'll serve us."

"Must be nice to be you. How does it feel to snap your fingers and have everything handed to you on a silver platter?"

After a moment of silence, he said, "It feels great. It was especially nice Friday afternoon, when the Liggetts crashed into my room and stuck a needle in me. Speaking of silver platters, maybe they'll bring us some more shrimp. I can starve to death while there's food right in front of me." His voice rose in hurt and anger. "It's great to be me, Reece. One of my gold-dusted moments was when Lester Oliver zapped you and I couldn't remember one damn thing about the CPR I learned in PE last year. It's great being me and being able to do nothing while they hurt you!"

Reece wanted to swallow back every word she had said. Christopher was her only ally in this mess, and she had hurt him. "I'm sorry." She reached for him. "I'm so sorry, Chris."

"It's Christopher and I can't help who I am."

His misery tore at her. She sought his hand in the darkness, found it, and she sat facing him. "I keep saying the wrong things," she murmured.

"Then don't say anything."

He was so close, she felt his warmth and inhaled his scent. The days were stifling hot in the dim airlessness of their prison, but the nights brought a chill that made the darkness as large and empty as a tomb.

"Christopher, I—"

"Shh." The syllable softly grazed her cheek.

"But—" she persisted.

He placed his hands on her knees. From there he found her forearms, her shoulders, and her face. His thumbs brushed across the cool, moist skin of her cheeks. She was getting better at hiding her tears. He might not see them, or even hear them, but he could always feel them.

"I'm not the kind of girl you date." She placed her hands over his. "I saw a picture of that heiress you went out with. It was in The Daley News."

Prescott alumnus and *St. Louis News-Chronicle* gossip columnist Katy Odenkirk had built a career reporting on Prescott families in her daily gossip column, The Gateway, in which The Daley News was a weekly feature. Katy's loftiest ambition in life seemed to be exposing the public to every aspect of Christopher's life. She had even written an unauthorized biography: *Daley 3: The Billion Dollar Boy*.

"Katy Odenkirk is a ferret-faced sucker fish," he said. "I don't know who's the bigger creep, her or her stupid brother

Larry."

"A ferret-faced suckerfish and a rancid goat turd," Reece said. "Their parents must be so proud."

"My date with that heiress was a one time thing," he told her. "Our handlers set it up. Her father wanted my father to purchase a minority interest in a shipping company based in Athens. I went horseback riding with her while our parents bumped heads about business. Neither of us knew that photographers would be photographing us from helicopters."

"I'm not sophisticated enough for you," she blurted.

"I'm not good enough for you."

His raw sincerity stunned her. Before she could argue to the contrary, the bare overhead bulbs flooded the room in a wash of light that pierced their eyes. The door burst open. Reece jumped, and Oliver and the Liggett brothers sauntered in. Christopher stood and hover protectively over Reece.

The Liggetts wore their usual attire: dirty jeans, mud-encrusted work boots and sweat-stained, faded T-shirts. In sharp contrast, Oliver wore a smart tuxedo, his light brown hair styled to perfection. Despite his luxe attire, his pale eyes and weak features still bore the look of an ill-tempered backwoodsman.

"You look disgraceful," Oliver told Christopher. He sniffed in disgust. "Augie would be mortified to see what's become of you."

"Did you enjoy the Booster Fundraiser?" Christopher asked calmly. Even in his dirty clothes and with two days' stubble roughening his face, he possessed a dignity that rebuffed Oliver's insults.

"I wouldn't have missed it for the world," Oliver sighed longingly. "All that money in one room. It was breathtaking. I was seated only three chairs from the governor. I overheard him asking your father about you."

Oliver pinned his gaze on Reece. She felt so exposed, sitting, in the middle of the floor, shaking. Christopher's left hand grazed her hair, and that small gesture kept her from bursting into hysterical screams.

"Your father, consummate liar that he is, announced that you were spending the Labor Day weekend with family back East, on Martha's Vineyard. I'm afraid your parents just weren't having a very good time at the function," Oliver continued, delighting in his cruelty. "Augie made his excuses early. He left in the middle of the luncheon, after the scholarship recipients were introduced. He didn't go far, however. He and your mother are holing up in the penthouse at the Janus."

Like a hungry jackal, Oliver circled Christopher. Reece shuddered, the chattering of her teeth providing weird music for Oliver's footfalls.

He spoke with the ersatz Harvard accent he'd affected since graduating from Winterhill College. "D.I.I. spared no expense in turning out twelve of Missouri's finest high school seniors. I was a Booster candidate sixteen years ago, Christopher. Has your father ever mentioned that? Augie himself interviewed me during a luncheon at The Rise."

He stopped pacing. Ross squatted, resting his elbows on his thighs as he gnawed the stained end of a toothpick. Gentry stood with his back pressed to the wall. He looked as if he had recently finished crying or would start any second.

"Your father completely fascinated me," Oliver said, his gaze fixed dreamily on a gouge in the floor. "He was dressed so very well and he radiated power and wealth. So much wealth, and he hadn't earned a single penny of it."

He snapped his steely gaze back to Christopher. "I wasn't awarded a scholarship. I suppose didn't make a good enough impression. Perhaps I even embarrassed him. You see, I didn't know which fork to use for the salad or fish. I slurped my soup. I believe I actually tucked my napkin into the waistband of my pants." He laughed bitterly. "It's no wonder Augie didn't believe me worthy of a Booster.

"That lunch with your father showed me a whole new world, one I longed to join. I got into college without your father's help, and I excelled. I got a degree in business, but I majored in D.I.I. I studied your family's history. After I graduated, I interviewed at D.I.I. four times, until I got a job in the public relations department."

Christopher yawned. "This is supposed to interest me…why?"

"You were only a child when I came aboard, Christopher. You were a sniveling, obnoxious brat interrupting meetings and throwing tantrums when you didn't get your way," Oliver sneered.

"I was a five-year-old with a father who thought it was never too early to learn the family business," Christopher muttered.

"You were a constant reminder to us all that you were the one who would one day control D.I.I.," Oliver continued. "I remember a day when you were eight years old, crawling between the legs of our chairs like a giant rat. That was the first time I entertained the idea of kidnapping you, but integrity prevailed. It's rather low business to abduct a defenseless child. I pushed that idea aside and I actually believed I could prove my worth through diligence and hard work. But your father passed me over one time too many. He screwed me. Now, I'm going to screw back."

Christopher closed his eyes against a wave of dizziness that threatened to bring him to his knees. Low blood sugar was taking its toll.

"I can't wait to see Augie tomorrow, at the Labor Day Picnic," Oliver said blithely. "I guess he won't be competing in the Father-Son sack race." He made a showy gesture of caressing Reece's earlobe with the tip of his finger. She whimpered miserably. Oliver grinned, and began to squat before her.

"Maybe you'll get lucky," Christopher said quickly, stepping between Reece and Oliver, "and he'll choose you, Lester." He locked his jaw, tasting blood as he readied himself for Oliver's inevitable reaction.

Oliver whirled on him, grabbing Christopher's shoulders and violently driving a knee into his groin.

"Please, Mr. Oliver, don't hurt him!" Reece pleaded.

Christopher doubled over, his lungs emptied, pain filling his lower belly. Oliver smashed Christopher's face into his knee before shoving him to the floor at Reece's feet.

Sobbing, she reached for Christopher.

"Don't touch me!" he gasped, swatting at her hands through the blinding pain.

She scurried away and curled into a ball, tightly closing her eyes and pressing her hands to her ears. No matter what she did, she couldn't block out the sound of Oliver's glossy English shoes violently connecting with Christopher's body.

"What God gives so much to some and so little to others," Oliver spat, standing over Christopher and panting from his exertions. "You don't deserve the Daley fortune. You don't deserve *life*."

Ross laughed. Gentry took a step toward Reece, who skirted out of his reach, sobbing under her breath.

"I know you, Christopher. I know about your weekend trysts with Traci Corliss and I know about the thousands you've gambled away in Las Vegas and Atlantic City. You're a self-centered wastrel of no use to anyone." He squatted near Christopher's head. "One more thing—I know about your rent-a-geek and how he used the Janus computers to hack into Prescott, to change your final exam scores last semester."

Oliver stood and straightened his jacket. He patted his hair back in place. "You may very well be heir to the world, Christopher, but here in this room, you're less than nothing."

Chapter Eight

"Reece?"

"Reece."

His voice penetrated the anesthetizing sleep she reluctantly had fallen into. She opened her eyes to the dark of morning, but kept her face to the wall.

"Reece." His voice was so sharp and brittle it broke on her name. "I need the bathroom."

"You don't need my permission," she sulked.

"I need your help."

The events of the previous night flooded back to her. Their makeshift date. Oliver's rage. Christopher's rejection. Christopher's blood.

"Don't make me beg."

She scrambled over to him, her limbs stiff and heavy from her awkward sleeping position. He was on his side, his clothes filthy with dust and dried blood. He drew a sharp breath when she helped him sit up.

"Your skin is so cold," she said. "You feel like a statue."

All night, the chilly wind had whistled through the boards covering the windows. The heating vent in the ceiling had been blocked off with a piece of drywall. Cold had settled into Christopher's bones and his blood had pooled into frozen lakes in the muscles of his back and legs.

"I can't move," he said, eerily calm. "I woke up and I couldn't make my legs work."

She clapped her hands over her mouth, her tears spilling over them.

"I'm kidding," he lied. "I probably look worse than I feel."

"You look pretty bad." Reece whimpered.

"It doesn't hurt," he insisted. That was the biggest lie of all.

His untruths were exposed when he collapsed onto her after she helped him to his feet. Bearing most of his weight, she struggled with him into the bathroom. While Reece closed the door, Christopher braced his hand on the cover of the toilet tank to keep himself upright. Icy sweat beaded on his forehead.

He was lightheaded, and might have passed out if Reece's busy fingers hadn't shocked him into full consciousness.

"I can do the rest," he said hastily, but not before she finished unzipping his khaki trousers.

"Are you sure?" She suddenly didn't know what to do with her hands or where to look. "I can wait. I won't look."

"Are you scared to be alone in there?"

She nodded. Two tears coursed down her cheeks. He idly wondered how she could produce so many tears when she'd had so little to drink in the past two days.

He waited until she was standing at the other end of the narrow room before he finished opening his pants. Squinting tightly and gritting his teeth to keep from screaming, he emptied his bladder. Was he passing acid and splinters of glass? He opened his eyes and blanched at the deep, sunset-red water in the toilet bowl.

"I'm finished," he winced, biting his lip as he flushed.

She waited for him to fasten his pants before she slid an arm around him and helped him to the sink basin. He sat heavily on the rusted side of the overturned bathtub and then rested his forearms on the edge of the basin, his hands dangling into the bowl. He lowered his head to his forearms as the dank water ran over his hands.

"I'm sorry about last night," he said.

She sat beside him and used her teeth to tear at the one clean sleeve of the shirt he had discarded after she had retched on him.

"You don't have anything to be sorry about." She ripped the sleeve free, wet it, and used it to swab the sheen of perspiration coating his brow.

"I pushed you away."

She gently wiped blood from his forehead.

"I don't want them to know how much I care about you." It took a lot of effort for him to hold his head up. "Oliver would hurt you, just to hurt me, if he knew how much-"

She dabbed at the fresh cut on his chin. His skin was frighteningly pale beneath the scarlet wound and his new bruises. The stubborn streak of dried blood under his nostril took the longest to remove.

She was rinsing the sleeve when the most ungodly sound on earth blared into the room. It was a siren, its awesome noise rattling the whole house hard enough to shake dust from the air vent and rust from the underside of the basin.

Reece's nerves were already raw and frazzled, and the sudden wail of the siren pushed her beyond reason. She screamed. She threw her head back, screaming so hard that the cords of her neck stood out against her skin. Even then the siren entirely masked the sound she made.

The siren went on forever, then ended as abruptly as it had begun.

In the deafening silence, Christopher's blood pounded in every injured part of his body. The siren had been yet another assault, inflicting a new kind of agony.

The soft noise that followed the blare of the siren was even more frightening. Someone was knocking on the bathroom door.

Reece hiccoughed on her tears as Christopher struggled to his feet and limped to the doorway. He gripped the knob so hard, it creaked in his hand as he pulled the door open.

Reece bit her fist to stop herself from screaming again.

It was only Gentry. His left eye was purple and swollen to the size of a golf ball. He looked Christopher over with his good eye, whistling under his breath.

"You shore went and made Les- I mean, Leighton, good an' mad las' night. Why'd ya hafta go an' call 'im Lester? Ain't nuthin' he hates more'n bein' called Lester. Ross had to go an' tell 'im that I'm the one who tole' you his name." His pale fingers glanced off his injured eye as he backed away from the door. "Man, it sure is dark in here.

"Les…dang it! I mean Leighton, once knocked Ross's front teeth right outta his head, fer callin' 'im Lester one time too many," Gentry said. "You gotta be as crazy as mud lizard to go after a dump truck like Ross. He got kicked out of wrestling school for puttin' a feller in the hospital with one punch."

The aroma of warm bacon drew Reece from the bathroom. Gentry pointed to a white, grease-stained paper bag on the floor. The bag's contents had very recently been deep-fried, and the scent was the only force on earth capable of overriding Reece's fear.

"Food," she said, eagerly kneeling over the bag. "It's food!"

"Lester...tarnation! I mean Leighton, he give us some money 'afore he went back to the city las' night. Ross is still sleepin', so I went an' got y'all some grub. I bet y'all are real hungry. Dixie makes the best dang flapjacks I ever had. Her place is down the road a right piece, but I expect it's still good 'n hot."

Reece tore the bag apart and ripped open a clear plastic container filled with flapjacks that were the approximate size and shape of dinner plates. She shoved an entire flapjack into her mouth, stuffing it in with all ten of her fingers. After a few cursory chews, she swallowed.

"I don' know how Ross sleeps through that blasted siren." Gentry fidgeted nervously with his belt loops, conversing as though they were all old friends. "Long as we done lived here, he could sleep right on through it. The dang thing goes off at the auto plant every Monday through Friday, even on Christmas. The plant's been closed for near 'bout six years now, so I don' know why nobody flips the switch on it so folks can sleep past eight through the week."

"Don't you have to get up for work anyway?" Christopher asked.

"Naw." Gentry picked at a scab on his elbow and elaborated. "There ain't been work around here since the plant shut down. Ross had twelve years in and figured on stayin' 'til he earned his pension. He was gonna get me somethin' there, too, after I finished up at Juniper Falls High. I missed the boat by six weeks."

"So you and Ross earn a living by kidnapping people," Christopher suggested.

Reece slowed her eating, her gaze darting between Christopher and Gentry.

Gentry brayed with laughter, revealing a mouthful of decaying teeth. "No, we ain't never done nothin' this big before! Ross boosts cars and handles jobs for a fella down Jefferson City. The pay is good and he likes roughin' folks up, but he'd still rather be fighting in Wrestlemania."

"What about you?" Christopher asked. "Isn't there something you'd rather be doing than this?"

Gentry stared at his feet for a moment. "I always wanted my own fix-it shop. I wasn't never much good at books and stuff at school, but I can fix near 'bout anything with a motor. The last time Ross was sent down BCC, I built him a tattoo gun hidden inside a clock radio. He sold it to another con and got all his ink done for free. He's got a Chinese dragon on his back that looks like it's breathin' real fire!"

"What's 'BCC'?" Reece asked warily.

"Boonville Correctional Center."

"What was he in for?" Christopher asked.

"A fight." Gentry's smile faded. "He tore up a fella at a bar. The guy died and Ross got pinched for involuntary manslaughter. He served two years outta the fifteen he got. He'd still be there if Lester hadn't got him a real good lawyer from up St. Louis. A few weeks later, Lester asked him for help with you."

"What did he do for you?" Christopher asked, a hard edge to his voice.

"I don't follow you."

Christopher's nostrils flared in his struggle to keep his cool. "For kidnapping me. What did Lester Oliver do for you?"

"Nothin', far as I know," Gentry replied, his blue eyes wide. "Ross asked me to help," he shrugged. "He's my brother. I had to help 'im."

"You could help him more by going to the police and turning yourself in," Christopher said. "End this before anything worse happens."

Gentry chuckled, but fear sprang into his eyes. "No, that ain't a good idea at all, not if I want to keep breathin'. Ross would beat the hell outta me first chance he got, but he's always careful not to kill me. Lester ain't close like me 'n Ross. That evil sumbitch would put a hole in my head and ditch me in a sewage pipe."

Reece gagged. As hungry as she was, her stomach wasn't ready for her gluttony and the unexpected onslaught of carbohydrates.

Gentry touched her shoulder. "You all right, Miss Reece?"

His fingers had barely lighted on her when she jumped. Her right fist shot out and caught him in his gut, knocking him halfway across the room.

"Don't touch me!" she shrieked. "Don't you ever, ever touch me!"

"I'm sorry, I'm so sorry!" Gentry cried. He scrambled away from her, holding his hands protectively over his face.

Fueled by the flapjack and her volcanic anger, she attacked the weakest link in the chain binding her and Christopher.

"You're sorry? That's all?" she raged. "Sorry for drugging me? For beating Christopher and electrocuting me and starving us? You're sorry all right, you backwards son of a bitch! Get out of here before I rip your head off! Get out!"

Terrified, Gentry skittered out of the room and slammed the door. The deadbolt slid into place behind him.

Reece turned to see Christopher standing behind her. She wondered if she had actually scared Gentry off, or if Christopher's presence had.

Whichever, she was just glad he was gone.

She helped Christopher lie down, and she took off her sweater to pillow it beneath his head.

He turned his cheek into her sweater. It smelled like her, sort of flowery and warm, with an earthy, spicier undertone. A symphony of pain played throughout his body, but each inhalation of her scent lessened the intensity of each crescendo.

"I've got some ibuprofen in my bag," she offered, searching for it. "It's the generic brand that Halgreth's Pharmacy sells, but my mom says the generic is made of the same stuff as the name brand." She found the small white bottle and popped the cap with her thumb. After pressing two caplets to his mouth, she opened a bottle of orange juice and held it to his lips.

"We have food," she said. "I know that there are people who have to go a lot longer than two days without a proper meal, but I'm so hungry."

Christopher fought to keep his eyes open. As tousled and dusty as she was in jeans and a plain white T-shirt, he wanted to look at her for as long as he could. The scarce light would fade only too soon.

"Try to save something for me," he said softly. "Unless there's shrimp in it."

"You have to eat." She finished unpacking the bag.

"I can't, not right now." The juice had felt like fire against the fresh cut on his lip.

His words were so stilted and quiet, the rustling of the bag drowned them out. She abandoned their first real meal in two days to stroke his thick, dark hair from his face. The tender gesture brought moisture to his eyes.

"You have to eat something," she said quietly. "You'll get sick if you don't."

Getting sick was the least of his worries. He was much more concerned about what would happen to Reece if—the 'if' wasn't worth thinking about. Not yet.

"Oh, God," she moaned. "Your upper canine tooth is missing."

"Do you see it anywhere?"

She frantically looked around. "No."

"I was pretty sure that I swallowed it."

"You're so calm." Her voice quivered. "How can you be so calm?"

"It's one of the rules." He licked his lips. They were very dry and tasted salty.

"Rules?" She brought the orange juice to his mouth again. He drank it, wincing as it passed over his injured lip.

"Do what they say. Don't fight back. Await rescue. Kidnap Etiquette 101."

"Well, there doesn't seem to be a rule against eating, and

you need your energy." She tore open a carton containing a bumpy pile of scrambled eggs. Another carton held a heap of golden fried potato cubes. There were also four pieces of plain toast wrapped in wax paper. Reece took one and held it to his mouth.

He turned his head. "I'm not hungry, Reece. I just want to go to sleep."

"No," she said weakly. "Eat."

"I'm not mad at you, if that's what you're thinking. I'm just tired."

"Don't go to sleep," she begged.

"I didn't rest well last night."

"I'm not stupid. You don't have to lie to me."

"Have your breakfast."

"I know you're hurt," she blurted.

"It's just skin. It will heal."

"I saw the blood. Before you flushed, I saw the blood."

"You said you weren't going to look."

"I didn't, not at you, and I didn't mean to look in the first place." She sat on her heels, her hands covering her eyes. Her shoulders shook. "You can't go to sleep," she pleaded tearfully.

He finally understood. She didn't want him to sleep for fear he wouldn't wake up.

"How do you think Logan's party was?" He could barely hear the question, though it had come from his own mouth.

She sniffled. "I hope it was better than our date."

"It couldn't have been worse."

Watching the slow rise and fall of his chest, she nibbled a slice of toast. "Did you really change your grades?"

"My father threatened to send me to boarding school if I didn't get at least four As. I switched my B+ in Latin to an A. I switched it back after grades were mailed out."

"Mrs. Lindor never gives As," she said.

"You'd think my father would know that. He had Lindor for Latin when he was at Prescott."

She took a plastic fork from the bottom of the sack and pecked at the congealed scrambled eggs. "Are you still seeing

Traci Corliss?"

"I flew to New Orleans before school started to spend the weekend with her at Tulane. I haven't seen her since."

Traci Corliss was the resident sex diva of last year's senior class. She had gone through younger boyfriends the way other girls went through doorways. Reece and the other junior girls had stood by, totally powerless, as Traci worked her way through some of the choicest junior boys. Griffin Leary, Martin Sunwoo, Brendan Carpenter, Corin Lemmon, Ben Weatherly and Camden Dougherty had succumbed, in that order, to Traci's ample charms through the school year.

Reece knew exactly how ample Traci's charms were, as the well-endowed Miss Corliss had the habit of prancing about buck naked in the locker room.

"Traci called me the day after last year's prom," he said. "She wanted to go out."

"She was seeing Camden then, right?" Reece said. Camden was a total god. How could Traci possibly have chosen between the honeyed good looks of Camden Dougherty and the sable handsomeness of Christopher Daley III? That was like Eve choosing between a Red or Golden Delicious.

"Traci said Camden wouldn't put out."

"Really?" She didn't know Camden very well, but he had just earned her respect. "I suppose you did?"

"She wanted it. I wanted it. So…"

"You did it."

"We were both consenting adults."

"You may have been consenting, but you aren't an adult. You're a kid, an eighteen-year-old *kid*. Maybe that's your problem. You think you're all grown up because you drink wine and have sex, but you're not."

"Are you upset because I'm a 'kid,' because I had sex, or because I had sex with Traci?"

"It's your body, Chris."

"Christopher."

"If you want to treat it like the drive-thru at Tio Taco, that's your business. I'll never have sex with someone I don't love."

"How do you know that I don't love Traci?"

A lump of scrambled egg lodged in her throat. "Do you?"

"No."

"Did you?"

"The bonus question," he muttered. "No. I never loved her. I don't think I ever even liked her."

"How could you have sex with someone you don't like?"

"You'll understand once you've had sex."

"Don't patronize me, Chris."

"It's Christopher, and I wasn't."

"I never liked Traci, either. She's one of those people who'd be ugly if she didn't have money to buy skin treatments and nose jobs and designer clothes cut to flatter her weird figure. She's got a piggy nose, biscuit cheeks, and boobs the size of volleyballs. I never understood why so many guys were attracted to her, until Courtney Miller told me that Traci was a human party favor. Why don't you like her?"

"She's demanding, manipulative, selfish, rude, greedy, and snobby. And she has the most annoying laugh. It sounds like a pack of hyenas falling down a flight of wrought iron stairs." He winced, either from the memory of Traci's heinous laugh or the pain in his lower back.

"Did she dump you or did you dump her?"

"It was mutual. She's seeing her Art Appreciation professor, and I'm interested in someone else."

She ate a slice of cold bacon. Her stomach roiled.

"Reece?"

"Yes?"

"I told you I wasn't good enough for you."

Chapter Nine

Mrs. Daley sat at her vanity table, her head in her hands. She had given up trying to apply liquid liner to her upper eyelid. Her hands were too shaky to do anything other than open and close and turn fretfully over one another.

Mr. Daley silently appeared behind her, hugging her and pressing his cheek to hers. Her skin was as cool and soft as the satin of her dressing gown. He spoke the first neutral thought that came to his mind. "It's a beautiful day for the picnic."

She bristled out of his embrace. "Is it? I hadn't noticed. I haven't had time to appreciate the weather, Augie, because my son is missing. He was taken from me, and I can't do anything to help him. He could be dead, and the person who took him says that I have to go to the 50th Annual D.I.I. Labor Day picnic today, to maintain an appearance of normalcy." She grabbed desperate handfuls of her husband's white shirt. "I want my son! I want my Christopher!"

Mr. Daley took her tightly in his arms. He cradled her head to his shoulder and cried tears of anger, frustration and fear. "We have to be strong for him, Nicki," he said, calling her by the nickname he hadn't used since their honeymoon. "We have to hold on, just until tomorrow. All we have to do is give them the money when and where they ask for it."

Mrs. Daley jerked away from him and paced the room on shaky legs. "For God's sake, do you really believe that anyone who would steal our son right from our home will return him? You're a businessman! Can't you smell how rotten this deal is?" Her eyes gleamed with a frighteningly somber light.

"Don't say it, Nicki," he pleaded.

"We may never see Christopher alive again," she stated flatly, as if the very thought had killed her soul.

He dropped heavily onto the plush stool at the vanity table. She had voiced the one thought that had tormented him since the viewing of the ransom threat. Knowing she thought the same thing made the possibility of losing Christopher more real. "I'm calling the police." He reached for her cell phone on the vanity. "Wyndham was right. I should have gone to the authorities already."

"No!" Mrs. Daley cried, pulling the phone from his hand. "Don't. We can't."

"Do we really have anything to lose?"

She tightened her grip on his wrist. Tears glistened in her eyes. "He's not dead. We still have tomorrow to save him."

"How can you be so sure?" He kept his eyes on the phone. One call, and within five minutes he would have city, state, federal and international law enforcement agencies in a global manhunt for his son.

Mrs. Daley searched her husband's eyes for some sort of understanding. "I'd know if Christopher was already dead," she whispered. "If he were, I think I would be, too."

Craig Wyndham drove for over an hour in his customized van before he found a Catholic church with a wheelchair accessible entrance. The parking lot of St. Ursula's was empty, Labor Day not being a holiday that drew droves of worshipers. The church was old, its dark pine and rich velvet interiors illuminated by the deep reds, golds and blues cast by stained glass windows lining the east and west walls.

Mr. Wyndham didn't give the stunning windows a second glance as he wheeled himself to a confessional wide enough to accommodate his chair.

He had come to St. Ursula's to humble himself before God, to beg for the life of his daughter, to offer his own in exchange to bring Reece home. His heart turned to lead as he bowed his head. "Forgive me, Father, for I have sinned. It's been almost four years since my last confession."

"And why have you kept yourself from your faith for so long, my son?" responded the benevolent stranger on the other side of the musty partition.

"There was an accident," Mr. Wyndham said. "I'm confined to a wheelchair. I haven't been on speaking terms with God."

"You blame God for your accident?"

"No." Mr. Wyndham closed his hands into fists and his blunt fingernails bit into his calloused palms. Hot tears dropped onto his lap. "I blame my wife. She was recruited to teach at Prescott High School five years ago. She thought it would be a great opportunity for our girls. We left our home in Baltimore because of Sara. I was a firefighter here for a year when my last blaze left me in this chair."

"Are you certain you wouldn't have had an accident, or even been killed, in Baltimore? Yours is a dangerous occupation, regardless of where you practice. Do you truly believe that if you had stayed in Baltimore, you wouldn't have had the accident that left you in your chair?"

Tears striped the strong dark planes of Mr. Wyndham's anguished face, and he struggled to get out his next words. "My legs are nothing compared to something else I've lost because of Sara's job. If we had stayed in Baltimore, I wouldn't have lost one of my daughters."

Chapter Ten

Bailey was a great tennis player partially because she was a good runner. She ran out of her house, down Rankin Street and onto Brentwood Blvd. She stopped running almost three miles later, when she arrived at the front door of Evan Pruett-Fogharty's five-bedroom Colonial.

She rang the doorbell. When no one answered, she pounded the pristine white door with her fist and kicked at it with the toe of her sneaker.

"Alright, already!" nagged Evan's older sister as she opened the door. "Oh," Betsy said dully. She planted a hand on her hip. "You."

Unfazed that Prescott's head varsity cheerleader had sized her up and once again found her lacking, Bailey stepped around her and ran upstairs to Evan's room. She threw the door open. Magazines, their glossy pages littered with voluptuously naked women in impossible poses, flew under the bed, behind a bookcase, and out the window.

"Jeez, Bailey, can't you knock first?" Evan complained. Jesse Manolo and Spencer Bradford pulled their magazines from hiding and filed them in the plastic bin under Evan's bed.

Bailey's tear-stained face made the boys forget about the debauchery and depravity they'd planned to spend their holiday on. They swarmed around Bailey, who, despite being a girl, was their fourth musketeer.

"Bailey?" Jesse's black eyes glittered with concern. "What's wrong?"

"Nothing," she croaked in a futile attempt to follow her father's directive. "Everything," she admitted on a sob.

Evan cleared a space for her amidst the clutter of shirts, jeans, text books, Nerf balls, and half-eaten bags of chips and pretzels on his bed.

"What's the matter?" Spencer squatted in front of Bailey, a frown appearing between his dark brown eyes. "We thought you were doing that woman thing with Kyle today."

The boys grimaced.

Jesse pushed a tennis racquet to the floor and sat beside Bailey. Jesse's father was Cuban and his mother was a blonde, blue-eyed Brazilian. He had inherited his father's coloring, his mother's perfect features and the combined passions of both his hot-blooded parents. He squeezed Bailey's hand and searched her chocolate brown eyes. "Is it your dad again?"

Mr. Wyndham sometimes lapsed into moods so blue it seemed that the whole family would be swept away in a tsunami of melancholy. It had been nearly a year since his last plunge into the abyss of depression.

"Spit it out," Evan said. He had never seen Bailey cry, and he wasn't quite sure how to handle it. Betsy cried only when she wasn't getting her way. He had no idea how to handle genuine tears.

"I'm not supposed to tell," Bailey said in a pained whisper.

The boys looked at one another, then at Bailey. They never kept secrets from each other, not ever. They shared everything, especially their problems.

"Does it have something to do with why you didn't play Sunday afternoon?" Jesse asked.

Since ninth grade the foursome had played doubles every Sunday afternoon at Twin Lakes Country Club, where the Pruett-Foghartys were members.

"Anything you're not supposed to tell this much sounds like something you should tell," Spencer said sagely.

Even though Spencer had an identical twin, he was closer to the three people in Evan's room than he was to his own brother.

In a tearful, hushed confession, Bailey told them everything: about the kidnapping, the visit from the Daleys, even the ransom CD.

"Did you see the CD?" Evan asked.

The dark length of her ponytail bobbed as she shook her head. "The Daleys took it."

"Damn!" Jesse groaned. "We could have gotten fingerprints from it and taken it to the police, or traced it to the store where it was bought, or discovered the type of camera used to make it."

"Videotape is sold everywhere," Evan said. "Just about everybody's got a camcorder or a cell phone camera."

"The kidnappers were ballsy enough to go to her home," Spencer said. "I don't think they'd leave fingerprints on a tape."

"Man, this is too weird," Evan exhaled. "They took Christopher right out of his own house."

"That's balls," Jesse said.

"That's cold." Spencer shook his head. His long dreadlocks moved like willow fronds about his head.

Evan started for the door, carefully stepping over a set of barbells and islands of DVDs on the floor. "I haven't seen anything on television about this. I wonder if my dad knows anything."

Bailey leaped after him to block the door. Mr. Fogharty was managing editor of the *St. Louis News-Chronicle*. Determined to follow in his dad's footsteps, Evan was honing his reporting skills as editor of Prescott's school paper, the *Review*. "You can't tell anyone, Evan, especially your dad. They'll kill Reece and Christopher."

"I'll just casually ask my dad if he's heard anything." Evan wouldn't meet her eyes.

Jesse hurried forward and grabbed the front of Evan's shirt. "Christopher's a jerk, but do you want to get Reece hurt or killed?"

"Of course not!" Evan shoved Jesse away.

The boys might have come to blows if Spencer hadn't stepped between them.

"Evan, do you really think your dad would keep quiet about this?" Spencer said. "Think about it logically."

Evan wrestled with the question for a good thirty seconds before he looked at Bailey. The answer was in her eyes. "I won't say anything to anyone," he agreed grudgingly.

Jesse grabbed a plastic globe from the shelf above Evan's bed. The globe contained a baseball autographed by Ozzie Smith on the night of Smith's last game as shortstop for the Cardinals. It was Evan's most prized possession, even more treasured than the autographed ball he got on the night Cal Ripken Jr. of the Baltimore Orioles broke Lou Gehrig's record for the most consecutive games played.

Panic rose in Evan's eyes as Jesse tossed the globe to Spencer. "Swear on Ozzie," Jesse said.

"C'mon guys, this is an incredible story!" Evan protested.

Jesse grabbed the Ripken ball and tossed it to Spencer. "Swear, on Ozzie *and* Cal that you will never tell anybody about what we talked about in this room today," Spencer said.

Evan palmed each globe. "All right, damn it, I swear it. I won't tell anyone about the kidnapping."

Bailey breathed a sigh of relief and hugged him. Jesse and Spencer crowded around them.

"What do we do now?" Evan asked.

"Do what Bailey's doing," Spencer said, his heart breaking a little with each tear that fell from her eyes. "Act naturally."

"This is Kyle's day, Stirling," Taryn said sternly. "She doesn't want you here."

"Don't tell me where I can and can't be," Stirling growled. He would have grabbed her and dragged her to his car if they were any place other than on the front doorstep of her parents' house with Kelsey spying through the living room window.

"I want to know what's going on with Reece!" Stirling demanded, stabbing his thumb at his chest.

"Keep your voice down," Taryn said, her tone encouraging him to obey.

She placed her hand protectively over her abdomen. As the oldest Wyndham daughter, she had lent a hand in the rearing of each of her sisters, and Reece had been her first love outside her parents.

"This is so hard for everyone." She ran her hand over his chest. "Please, try to be patient. I'll call you as soon as we hear something."

He pushed her hand away, his black eyes flashing. "You're staying the night here *again*?"

She nodded, and he almost gave in to the urge to slap her. Once again the Wyndhams had closed ranks, drawing Taryn away from him. Celebrating Kyle's entry into womandom, or whatever the hell they called it, was one thing. Keeping him out of the loop of the story of the decade was another.

"I'm in a unique position to bring the kind of attention to this thing that could get Christopher and Reece home in a matter of hours," Stirling said.

Or get yourself a national spotlight, Taryn thought grimly.

"Remember Mark Klass?" he thundered. "And Fred Goldman? John Walsh didn't bend over and butter up. Those guys did something!" *And now people know their names,* he added to himself.

"Don't you dare say anything about this to anyone at KYNN," Taryn warned.

"Don't tell me what to do."

"You promised, Stirling."

"And you promised to love, honor, and obey me."

She squared her shoulders. Although she was smaller than her husband, she seemed to match him inch for inch, and muscle for muscle. "We've been married for six months and you've forgotten our wedding vows already. I promised to love, honor, and *respect* you. I have to tell you, babe, sometimes you make it very difficult for me to do any of those things."

He raised his hand. The rustle behind the living room curtains made him settle for crushing a handful of air.

"Go ahead," she invited with quiet, calm confidence. "Just remember that I know how to hit back."

Snorting like an overheated animal, Stirling backed off. He scowled at Taryn and got into his dark green Corvette. He left thick, black smears of burned rubber on Rankin Avenue as he zoomed away from the Wyndham home.

Chapter Eleven

"These eggs are like rubber," Christopher said, forcing them down.

"The potatoes have a bouncy texture, too."

"I might be eating your shoe for all I can tell. Actually, your shoe would probably taste better than this stuff."

"I'm glad you're feeling better." Reece genuinely meant that. Christopher had slept for a long time. She had watched him, her hand resting lightly, protectively, on his chest. The light was gone by the time he woke up so he had to eat cold leftovers in the dark.

"Do you have any of your mom's cookies left?"

There was one, which she gave to him.

He could sit up as long as he had the wall for support. The burning in his lower back had reduced to a tolerable simmer, thanks to her ibuprofen. She sat next to him, her side glued to his.

"What would you be doing today, if you weren't here," he asked.

"We usually have a barbeque. Today was supposed to be Kyle's day."

"Kyle. She's the youngest?"

"Yes."

"She goes to a special school, doesn't she?"

"You make it sound like she's retarded. She goes to the Scientia Center. It's for gifted kids. She's really smart."

"Today's her birthday?"

"No."

"Well, why is it Kyle's day?"

"You'll think it's stupid."

"Probably, but tell me about it anyway."

She pulled away from him. He almost fell over and passed out from the hot stabbing sensation that shot through his back. He hadn't realized that he'd been leaning on her so much.

"Comments like that explain why you have so much trouble making friends," she said coldly.

"Tell me about Kyle." He took deep breaths until the pain waned. "Please."

"Kyle got her first period Friday morning. It's a tradition for my mom and all of us girls to set aside a day to spend together, to sort of celebrate it. Today was Kyle's day. We were going to stuff our faces with White Castles and watch Kyle's favorite movies."

He was quiet for a long time. When he spoke, she thought he would say something obnoxious or insulting.

"What are her favorite movies?"

"She likes foreign films." She shifted position again. Christopher leaned on her to relieve the pressure on his back. "My mom got *Mediterraneo*, *Il Postino*, and *Like Water For Chocolate*."

"Kyle has great taste in movies."

"*Like Water For Chocolate* is my favorite. It's so rich and colorful and…and…"

"Sensuous?"

"Yes."

"Those are mature films for a little girl." His back felt even better when he hung his left arm across her shoulders and rested his head close to hers.

"Kyle isn't an ordinary little girl." She covered Christopher's forehead with her hand. "You're warm."

"So are you." He wanted to fall asleep again.

"No, I mean you're really hot. And you're perspiring." She cupped his face and touched her lips to his forehead. "You have a fever."

"Does that really work?"

"What?"

"Kissing someone to tell if he has a fever."

"That wasn't a kiss." She was glad they were in the dark. He couldn't see the heat climbing into her cheeks. "I'm afraid to give you more medicine. I don't know how long it's been since I gave you the last dose."

"Stop worrying about me, Reece. Think about tomorrow, when you'll be safe at home."

"You'll be home, too," she reminded him.

"Yeah," he said softly. "Me, too."

"What would you have been doing today?"

"Either recovering from the hangover I'd have earned if we had gone to Logan's party after the concert, or working on creating one at the D.I.I. picnic. It's the one day of the year that my parents and I put on the loving family act for the public."

"Your dad is probably going nuts worrying about you."

"My father is probably at the ballpark with his vice presidents lined up to kiss his ass. I'm the last thing he's worried about."

"Is something troubling you, sir?"

"I'm sorry, what?" Mr. Daley looked up to see his vice president of consumer relations staring down at him. He vaguely knew his vice presidents by sight, but with forty-two veeps spread over twenty departments, he knew them better by number, and he struggled to remember number 10's name.

"You look distraught, sir. Is there something with which I can help you?" Number 10 took a seat, making himself comfortable in the Daley luxury box. He motioned for the waiter to bring him another draft beer.

The picnic was the ultimate father and son fantasy. D.I.I had rented the Cardinals and their stadium for the day, giving the employees the chance to hit and run with major league ball players and to collect autographs. Parents, the fathers in particular, enjoyed themselves even more than their children.

Mr. Daley absently watched number 12's eight-year-old son learn to pitch a slider.

"It's the perfect day for a picnic, sir," number 10 persisted.

Mr. Daley threw an annoyed glance at him. "Yes. You should be out there on the field, enjoying it."

"As should Mrs. Daley. Is she not well? She's never missed a company picnic as long as I've been—"

"My wife's health is none of your concern, Oliver," Mr. Daley snapped, number 10's name coming to him in a flash of anger. He abruptly rose from his chair. "Excuse me. I have a pressing matter to attend to."

Leighton Oliver, the former Lester Oliver also known as number 10 and vice president of D.I.I. consumer relations, moved into Mr. Daley's vacated seat. "Of course, you do," he muttered smugly. "You very well do."

"Five minutes, that's all I need."

Stirling sat beside the news director in the KYNN station manager's office after pitching an idea to the head honchos. He'd managed to keep his solemn promise for twenty-nine hours.

He barely concealed his excitement behind a flimsy mask of concern. This kidnapping could do for him what war reports did for network reporters!

"There hasn't been a kidnapping this big since the Lindbergh baby got snatched!" he added.

"Girls like your sister-in-law are abducted by the dozens every day," said the jaded news director. "She's cute, she's young, she's local and she's a track star, but we can't open a broadcast with her."

Stirling leaned across the news director's desk and went for the kill. "Christopher August Daley III was the target. Reece is just along for the ride. Give me the air. KYNN will go down in history as the station that broke the Billionaire Boy kidnapping." Stirling sat back in his chair with a contented smirk.

"You have your five minutes," the station manager said. "You can have the top of the five o'clock broadcast."

Chapter Twelve

"Taryn and her big idiot husband want to combine their names to create a name for their baby," Reece said.

"What's the big idiot husband's name?" Christopher asked.

"Stirling."

"They could call the kid Staryn," he suggested. "Or Tarling."

"Yuck."

"If we had a baby we could call him Creese."

She didn't say anything.

"That was supposed to be funny."

"It was." She began to cry.

He pulled her into his arms as well as he could without hurting his back.

"I'd never have a kid with you," she sobbed.

"Why not?"

"Because then I'd have two babies on my hands."

"Oh, that was funny." He tickled her. "That was very funny."

Laughing, she wriggled away from him.

"You realize that for us to have a baby, we'd have to have sex," he said.

"I'm waiting until I'm married."

"Reach the point of no return after you've reached the point of no return, huh?"

"What?"

"What happens if on your wedding night, your true love turns out to be less than satisfactory between the sheets?"

"I won't marry someone stupid or cold. I certainly won't marry someone without an imagination."

"So you're hoping he'll be as inexperienced as you are."

"I read books," she said in her defense. "I watch cable, you know. My mom tells me anything I want to know. There are ways to learn about sex besides jumping into bed with every Harry, Dick and Tom—"

"I think you mean Tom, Dick and Harry," he laughed.

"—and Traci," she said pointedly.

He kept laughing.

"You're such a stinkoid."

"You're such a virgin."

"How old were you, the first time you did it?"

"Thirteen. It was with an au pair who took care of my cousins. She was eighteen. I told her that I was sixteen."

"What country was she from? Dumbland? The United States of Stupidity? She couldn't tell that you were just a kid?"

"I was big for my age."

"Really," she said dryly.

"Oh, I was really big."

"I get the picture. Thanks."

"I was so big that—"

"Christopher!"

"—she thought I was seventeen," he finished innocently.

"You're so perverted."

"You're so beautiful."

She was speechless.

"I'm sorry, I didn't mean to say that."

"You don't have to apologize for saying things like that, Chris, even if they aren't true."

"It's Christopher and I wouldn't have said it if it wasn't tr—"

The door crashed open and the light flared, startling them half out of their skins. He pushed her away, but not before she felt the tension in his body as her fingertips fell away from his.

Ross stormed into the room. Christopher's eyes closed, then slowly opened. He took a deep breath and steeled himself for what would come. Reece's toes curled and bunched against the soles of her running shoes. Her fingers tried to drive themselves through the roughened floorboards.

She must have made some sound, or perhaps it was the pounding of her terrified heart, because Christopher stirred. He lifted his head and threw his shoulders back. The pain of his movements showed in each of the new lines on his face as he got to his feet. He fought the urge to grab his middle, where

Oliver had probably cracked a couple of his ribs, and he stood up straight, despite the piercing, heated pain in his back.

Reece couldn't see Christopher's face, but she saw Ross's. He looked angry enough to take a bite out of Christopher.

"Your old man always gotta be the boss, don't he?" Ross boomed, spittle flying from his lips. "Always gotta have things his way!"

Christopher responded with unerring calm. "I don't have the slightest idea what you're talking about."

Ross slammed Christopher into the wall and pinned him there by his throat. "He warn't s'posed to tell nobody!" Ross's thin lips pursed as he stuck out his chin and curled his left hand into a fist the approximate size of a canned ham.

Christopher squeezed his eyes shut. Reece choked back a scream.

"Don't!" Gentry hollered, hanging from Ross's drawn fist with both hands. "Leighton gonna be mad enough already. He's gonna be downright nasty if'n he comes back an' sees that you done kil't 'im!"

Oliver's name seemed to be Ross's release command. He put his fist away and let go of Christopher, letting him sink to the floor before spitting at him. He winked at Reece before he shook off Gentry and left the room with him.

"Christopher?" Reece waited until the darkness returned before she lifted his arm and draped it across her shoulders to ease him into a sitting position.

"I don't know what any of that was about," he said wearily. "Obviously—"

"Something bad happened," she finished for him.

"I think you'd better come see this, Mr. Daley," said Eleanor Davenport, Mr. Daley's executive secretary.

"What is it, Eleanor?" he asked, following her into the main room of the luxury box, where the KYNN five o'clock news broadcast was underway. D.I.I. owned KYNN. When a few people had wanted to catch the evening news, KYNN was the obvious choice.

The large rectangular head and square shoulders of sportscaster Stirling Barton filled the wall-mounted flat-screen television behind the bar, and his voice filled the luxury box.

"—very concerned about the welfare of Christopher August Daley III, but my sister-in-law, Reece Wyndham, was also abducted." Stirling paused dramatically, a benevolent half-smile drooping above his chin. "Reece is a beautiful girl and a champion runner. Her mother, father, sisters and I miss her very, very much. Please study the photos on the screen. If you have any information about the kidnapping of Christopher August Daley III and Reece Wyndham, contact the KYNN Information Hotline at the number on your screen." He took a deep breath, touched his thumb and forefinger to his eyes. "Thank you, and God bless."

"Thank you, Stirling, for that touching plea for the safe return of Christopher Daley and your niece," said the silver-haired co-anchor at the news desk.

"Sister-in-law," Stirling corrected icily.

"Our prayers are with these two families tonight," the blond anchorwoman added somberly. She brightened as she said, "Stirling Barton will return later in the broadcast with the KYNN Sports Report and highlights from the Red Birds series-opening trouncing of the Cubs."

A car commercial came on and everyone in the box turned to Mr. Daley.

It took him a long moment to compose a reaction. "This is pure nonsense," he finally said, surprising himself with how convincing he sounded. "Christopher is visiting friends on Cape Cod. Mrs. Davenport, get the station manager on the line, I—"

Mrs. Davenport stood at his side with the phone in her hand. There was already an urgent call on his private line. He took the phone into the room where Mrs. Daley was resting, thanks to a little help from Prince Valium.

Mr. Daley held the phone in both hands for a moment before he brought it to his ear. "Daley, here," he said, his voice breaking.

"The man himself! How are you, Augie?" said the chipper female voice on the other end of the line. "Katy Odenkirk here. I was wondering if you'd like to comment on a story I'm breaking in a special edition of The Daley News tomorrow."

"I have nothing to say to you," he said tersely.

"Where's Christopher?" Katy demanded.

"He's on the Cape. With friends." Mr. Daley hung up the phone. He sat on the edge of the bed and gently shook his wife until she woke up. "We have a problem, Nicki. The Wyndhams went on the air about the kidnapping. The Wyndhams went to the media!"

Chapter Thirteen

Leighton Oliver was on the field having his photograph taken with two Cardinal outfielders and the shortstop when a beeper went off. "It's mine," he said as each of the ball players and the photographer reached for their pagers. Oliver glanced at the digital readout. The number was 876-8253. TRO-UBLE.

"Stirling Barton had no right, and certainly no authorization from anyone in this house, to do what he did!" Craig Wyndham shouted into the phone.

"That doesn't change the fact that reporters are hounding me at every turn!" Mr. Daley yelled. He paced before the glass wall of the penthouse as he railed at Mr. Wyndham. "How am I supposed to transfer the ransom while the eyes of the world are watching every move I make? Tell me that, Craig. Better yet, why don't you ask that stupid son-in-law of yours."

"Have you heard from them?"

"The kidnappers?"

"No, Lady Di and Mother Theresa," Mr. Wyndham snarled. "Of course, the kidnappers!" There was an urgent female voice in the background at the Wyndham house. "Would you just shut up for a minute, Sara?" Mr. Wyndham snapped before returning to Mr. Daley.

"No, I haven't heard from them," Mr. Daley said.

"Call me when you do." Mr. Wyndham slammed down the phone.

Oliver sat on a gray metal folding chair. He faced Christopher and Reece, who also sat on folding chairs. Oliver was torn. He couldn't decide who to blame for the temporary setback in his master plan.

Stirling Barton was Reece's brother-in-law, but Augie Daley owned KYNN. Perhaps it had been a collaborative effort. No matter how it had happened, someone had to pay.

Beads of sweat ran down Christopher's face as he squirmed, trying to find a little comfort for his back against the hard metal. Reece gripped the rust-splotched edges of her seat. She was too tense with fear to do anything but stare at Oliver's boat shoes.

"Eenie, meanie, mynie, moe," he said, lazily dragging his forefinger through the air to point alternately at Christopher, then Reece. "Catch a tiger by the toe." He paused to grin at his cousins.

"If he hollers, let him go," Oliver continued. "Eenie. Meanie. Mynie." His finger hung in the air inches from Reece's nose. "You."

He rested his elbows on the knees of his crisply pressed linen trousers and leaned toward her. "When I asked you about your family, you failed to mention your brother-in-law and the fact that he's on-air talent for KYNN. I can't help but wonder why you would have neglected to mention your family tree's most fascinating fruit."

She opened her mouth to explain but only pips and squeaks of air came out. Oliver hooked his forefinger under her chin and lifted her face, bringing it level with his. Dark lilac circles tinted the tender skin beneath her shimmering eyes. Her cheeks were a bit gaunt and smudged with dust, and her lower lip trembled. "It's perfectly all right, Reece. This will be over soon." He ran the pad of his thumb over her chin.

"Obviously my father was behind whatever happened," Christopher blurted. "Leave Reece alone."

"Like father, like son." Oliver motioned toward Ross. "Always giving orders."

Armed with a thick roll of silver duct tape, Ross and Gentry came at them. Christopher cried out in pain when Ross clapped an arm across his chest, holding him in place while Gentry taped his arms and legs to the chair.

Oliver grabbed the seat of Reece's chair and pulled her closer, until her knees were between his. "Why didn't you tell me about Stirling Barton?"

"He's my sister's husband," she said meekly, listening to Christopher's agonized noises and the ripping tape behind her.

"He's not real family."

"Do I detect a note of dislike directed toward your brother-in-law?"

"I hate him."

He recoiled from the potency of her answer. "Oh? Why is that?" He brought his face close to hers and ran his tongue over his lower lip. "He seems to care a very great deal about you. Enough to throw your life away."

"He doesn't care about anyone but himself and what's between his legs."

Oliver sat back in his chair. "Oh, Reece, you poor, put upon little thing. Did your boorish brother-in-law put the moves on you?"

Her face reddened.

"That's it, isn't it," he said with mock tenderness. "Is that why he wants you back?" He cupped the back of her head in one hand. "So he can feel your silky hair between his fingers?" He traced her cheekbone with a fingertip. "And touch your creamy skin?" He stared at her mouth. "Or feel these lovely lips wrapped around his—"

"Leave her alone!" Christopher shouted, struggling against the tape just as Reece lashed out, slamming her cupped hand against the left side of Oliver's head. He grabbed his ear and doubled over. The blow caught him perfectly, and it felt as if his eardrum had been pierced with an ice pick.

"Stirling Barton is a bastard and I hate him!" Reece screamed. "I hate him as much as I hate you!"

Oliver staggered away from her and sneered, "Thank you for making what I have to do so much easier." He pinned his gaze on Gentry, who cringed by the door. "Get the needle."

Gentry's head moved slowly from side to side. "It almost kil't her las' time," he whined pitifully.

"That's the idea!" Oliver hollered.

Gentry left the room. Oliver grabbed Reece by her right shoulder and jerked her to her feet.

"Please, just leave her alone!" Christopher pleaded. "Whatever went wrong is my father's fault, I'm sure of it."

"How chivalrous of you, Christopher," Oliver said nastily. "Betray your father to save the damsel." He shoved Reece to Ross, who gladly fastened a thick arm around her waist and clapped a meaty hand over her mouth.

"Don't hurt her!" The tape tore Christopher's skin as he fought to free himself.

Oliver snatched up the roll of tape and slapped a piece of it across Christopher's mouth. "I'm not going to hurt her," he said evenly. "I'm going to kill her."

Christopher wriggled and pulled against the tape, grunting and squealing in anger.

Reece went boneless in Ross's arms. Oliver stood before her. "I know this comes as something of a shock, and I'd apologize if you hadn't deafened me in one ear."

Her eyes seemed to lose focus before drowsing shut.

Oliver snapped his fingers in her face and sharply smacked her cheeks to rouse her. "Don't leave us yet, Reece. I want you to know exactly what's going to happen to you, and why."

Her head lolled to face Christopher. He was still trying to free himself, his chest heaving and his eyes wild.

"Someone broke my most crucial directive," Oliver said. "Now I find myself forced to prove that I am deadly serious. I'm afraid Christopher is still useful to me. I can't collect my money without him." He touched the hollow of Reece's throat. "I've made other plans for you."

She stared unblinking, tears cutting through the grime dusting her cheeks. The tape sealed in Christopher's screams.

"When Gentry returns I'll give you an injection," Oliver explained. "You will fall into a deep, restful sleep. Your breathing will slow. Your heart rate will decrease. There's the possibility that you'll lapse into a coma. If, by morning, your heart still hasn't stopped, then Ross will finish you. Your undamaged, unmarked body will be left at The Meeting of the Rivers, that beautiful fountain opposite Union Station. Your corpse will be so fresh you'll look like you're sleeping. While the authorities and the media are in a feeding frenzy over your body, I'll be collecting my money. You see, your death is for the greater good. Mine." He smiled, and then kissed her forehead.

Gentry returned. Reece's eyes went to the syringe pinched in his fist. She pried Ross's hand from her mouth. "I don't want to die," she gasped.

"You mean you don't want to die today," Oliver corrected.

Reece loved her life so much that she found the strength to hold on to Ross's arms and drive her feet into Oliver's chest. Her momentum sent Ross crashing into the wall and his hold relaxed enough for her to fight her way out of it. Oliver had stumbled backward into Gentry, who'd hit the floor with a hard, noisy splatter. The syringe bounced from his hand and skidded across the floor.

Reece made a run for it. Oliver and Gentry blocked her path to the door. The floor shook from Ross's heavy steps behind her.

She went for the syringe. If she could stab one of them with it, she would. "No!" Gentry shrieked, beating her to it and clutching it to his narrow chest.

Ross tackled Reece and wrestled her to her knees. Oliver snatched the syringe from Gentry. Reece screamed and clawed at Ross as he wrenched her around to face Christopher. Oliver grabbed a handful of her hair, jerked her head to one side, and fixed his eyes on Christopher as he blindly plunged the needle into Reece's neck.

A high-pitched cry tore from her when the needle pierced her flesh. Almost immediately, the nerve-shattering sound stopped as cleanly as if it had been severed with a straight razor.

Christopher's struggles tapered off, then ceased as he watched her mouth work to form words, or another scream. Nothing came out as her arms dropped to her sides. Her body completely relaxed. Her eyelids drowsed shut once, twice, then closed and opened no more. Ross dragged her to a corner and left her there in a heap.

Oliver stepped in front of Christopher and slowly pulled the tape from his mouth.

"Damn you!" Christopher shrieked, hot tears obscuring his vision. "You killed her! How could you?"

"I didn't want *her* to suffer," Oliver said coldly.

Chapter Fourteen

A cold hand came through the darkness and touched his bare shoulder. He jolted awake, shivering, half on the floor and half in the chair.

Please don't! Please, don't! Please, please, please! The tape over his mouth sealed the pleas into his head.

"It's me." Reece's voice was directly in his ear. "It's only me."

Those were the sweetest words he'd ever heard as he tugged against the tape binding his hands to the chair. Her hands moved over his face, feeling for the end of the tape over his mouth. Perspiration had loosened the adhesive so the tape peeled off without removing much more of his skin.

A sound approximating her name climbed out of his raw throat.

She went to work on the tape at his wrists and ankles. He repeated her name over and over, the constant intonation steadying her nerves and her hands.

She freed him, eased him to the floor, and gathered him into her arms. His hair and skin were sticky and reeked of stale champagne, and he shivered even though his skin felt like he was being roasted from the inside out.

Reece had awakened to darkness. *I'm dead again,* had been her first thought, and the afterlife wasn't anything like she'd been taught. No angel choirs welcomed her into the light of God's eternal love. There was only darkness as oppressive and complete as she imagined Hell to be.

Her nose told her that she wasn't dead, although she was definitely in a kind of hell. The one she'd been taught to fear was supposed to smell like brimstone. This one smelled of bodily waste, ozone, stale liquor and cigar smoke.

The soft sound of stilted breathing had drawn her to Christopher. He had shuddered at her touch and made a woeful noise that had frozen her blood.

"I'm still here," she said, breaking his litany of her name.

His extremities ached as blood circulated to areas the tape

had cut off. Not to be outdone, the pain in his back roared to the forefront.

Her hands wandered over him and she discovered that he was naked, and that the sticky substance covering him was too thick to be perspiration. "Christopher," she began in a quivering voice, "what did they do to you?"

He tightened his arms around her waist and buried his face in her chest. Shivering, he tasted blood at the back of his throat and forced out the only word he uttered that wasn't her name. "Everything."

"It really reeks in here." She broke the silence they had endured since she found his trousers and helped him into them. Moving about had helped him, a little. He could sit up, as long as he rested against her.

"They were celebrating." His voice was hoarse. "Cigars, champagne...the works."

She swallowed hard. "When they come back, and I'm not dead..."

"Maybe you can fake it, until you get outside."

"And then what? When he pulls out the gun or puts those big fat hands around my throat I yell 'Boo!' and scare him to death?"

"You're a runner. That's your strength. Plus you'll have the element of surprise on your side."

"Gentry filled the syringe. Do you think he messed it up on purpose?"

"Who knows? He's not exactly the brains of this operation."

"They want to kill me, Christopher. All because of Stirling."

"Stirling just made it happen sooner."

"What?"

"Nothing."

"I was glad to wake up again, even if it was here," she said. "I don't want to die. Not ever. Three times is enough."

"Stirling hurt you, didn't he?"

"He got drunk at the rehearsal dinner the night before his wedding. He grabbed me as I came out of the ladies room. Before I knew what was happening, he slimed me up with a sloppy wet kiss. I think he would have tried more if I hadn't told him that I would tell Taryn. Afterward, I felt so angry and helpless that all I could do was cry my eyes out."

"You didn't tell anyone?"

"He was drunk."

"That's no excuse."

"You've never been too aggressive with a girl?"

"I've always had the opposite problem."

"Oh, of course. You're just so irresistible, girls just throw themselves at you."

"The Daley name is what's irresistible. That au pair I told you about, the one from Dumbland? We only did it once. A month later, she told my father that I'd gotten her pregnant. She tried to extort twenty-five thousand dollars from my dad. She went to the media with the whole thing. At first everyone was on her side, but then she got caught trying to falsify the results of a court-ordered pregnancy test. It was a pretty huge scandal, because of my age. I'm surprised you didn't hear about it."

"That was five years ago. I was living in Baltimore then."

"Do you wish you'd never left Baltimore?"

"I did for a while, after my dad's accident. But then I figured he could have gotten hurt anywhere. He came really close a few times in Baltimore. If we'd stayed there, I never would have been able to go to a school like Prescott.

"I'm glad we moved to Brentwood. Taryn got a Daley Booster and went to Northwestern the first year we lived here," she said proudly. "Going to Prescott has opened so many doors for us. If we still lived in Baltimore, Taryn probably would have married that ding-a-ling from Dundalk she was dating."

"It sounds like your older sister has bad taste in men."

"If that's what you want to call them," she yawned. "I'm so sleepy. This is better than the nausea I had last time, though."

"You can sleep, if you want to. I don't think they'll bother us again tonight."

"How can you be so sure?"

"Oliver said that he had to go back to St. Louis, for the final stage. Ross and Gentry were so drunk they could hardly walk. They won't be back tonight."

The siren woke Reece up but it was the sunlight flooding the bathroom that got her on her feet. She stepped over swollen cigar butts, empty champagne bottles and the shredded remnants of Christopher's T-shirt and boxer shorts as she entered the bathroom.

She squinted at the dust motes dancing in the beam of bright light angling into the room. She was drawn to the light as unerringly as a moth to a flickering flame.

Christopher stood on the side of the overturned bathtub holding the filthy louvered cover to the air duct.

"I borrowed your nail clippers," he said apologetically. With the ungainliness of an arthritic old man, he started to climb off of the tub.

She stepped into the light, either to help him or catch him. "Christopher," she gasped, reaching out to touch him.

He caught her wrists. "I broke your clippers. I'm sorry."

Nail clippers that had cost her sixty-nine cents at Halgreth's Pharmacy were the least of her concerns as she stared at Christopher's bare upper body.

The cigars had been used for more than just smoking. There were clusters of burns, each burn the approximate diameter of a nickel, on Christopher's chest, abdomen and forearms. There were three pairs of dart burns, just like the ones she had on her chest. He was so mottled with bruises, burns, cuts and dried blood, his skin looked like it had been tie-dyed.

"I used the nail file to loosen the screws holding it in place. I waited until the siren went off to pull the vent out, so they wouldn't hear it." He pushed the clippers into her hand. His fingernails were ragged, the ends of his fingers raw and bloody from working on the screws. "I don't know why I didn't think of this sooner. I'm sorry."

She blinked away the tears stinging her eyes. "It's okay." She gasped and covered her mouth with a trembling hand as her gaze landed on the blood-caked "10" that had been very neatly engraved just below the hollow of his throat.

"It's just skin," he reminded her. He turned to the square of light in the wall. "It's time to get you out of here, before they come for us."

"*We're* getting out of here."

"I won't fit. And I can't run. Something's wrong with my back. It hurts to walk, or even stand."

She leaned around him to look. Dried blood speckled his skin and darkened the seat of his pants. The left side of his lower back was grotesquely swollen, the skin taut, hot and threaded with fine red lines. Reece began to sob in earnest.

"I won't fit, either," she insisted, staring at the vent. "The hole is too small."

"No, it's not. It can't be. You have to get out of here before they come for you. Oliver said that you're not worth anything. Well, you're worth everything to me, and this is probably your only chance. You have to go."

"They'll kill you if I go," she tearfully argued.

"They'll kill you if you stay," he insisted. "I begged them to kill me last night." Tears welled in his eyes. "But nothing they did to me last night hurt as much as watching what they did to you. They're going to kill me, Reece. But they can't do it until after they get their money. I have a little more time. You don't."

"M-Maybe... maybe we can talk to them," she hoped anxiously. "We'll promise not to give the police their names, and we'll give them more money. My parents own their house. They could take out a mortgage on it. It's only worth a couple hundred thousand, but—"

He grabbed her shoulders and gave her a hard little shake. "You're the only chance I have to make it out of this!"

Her eyes drifted over the bruised and bloody landscape of his face, and they lingered on a thin line of dried blood that had originated in his right ear.

She turned toward the vent. The empty hole looked no

bigger than a large shoebox. The tin edging had deteriorated into brittle layers of rust, and broken cobwebs floated on the mild breeze. The breeze lured her from Christopher.

She climbed onto the side of the tub and looked through the hole. The world outside overwhelmed her senses. The colors stung her eyes. The aromas tickled her nose. She coughed on the purity of the air. Her eyes drank in the vibrant blue of the sky and the puffs of white clouds hanging in it. A two-lane blacktop highway cut through an endless cornfield as dark and richly green as summer itself. She took a deep breath, filling her lungs with the scents of damp earth and fresh corn.

"Reece," Christopher said.

She reluctantly turned back to the bathroom and saw her travel-sized bottle of sunscreen clasped in one of Christopher's hands.

"I could go faster in a pair of shorts," she said nervously as he slicked her bare arms and legs with sunscreen. "At least I'm wearing my good shoes."

She'd been too bulky for her first attempt through the hole, so she'd stripped down to her sports bra and panties. A protruding nail head had torn through her jeans and snagged her half in and half out of the vent. If Christopher hadn't pulled her back she would have been stuck until the Liggetts came and found her there. It would have been like shooting fish in a barrel.

The effort it took to smear the suntan lotion on her took its toll on Christopher, but he insisted that she keep her hands clean. She would need a good grip to lower herself twenty feet to the ground.

"This would be a lot more fun if we were on a private beach in the Riviera," he said in an attempt to lighten the gravity of the situation.

His comment made her blood rush even faster than the prospect of being killed in an escape attempt. Her cheeks flushed and her heart beat faster with something other than fear for the first time since Friday afternoon.

"Is that an invitation?" she asked.

He turned her around to cover her back with sunscreen. "It's a promise." His hands glided over her shoulders and upper arms, thickly coating them with lotion.

"I'm scared."

The heat radiating from his fevered body baked her back. He spoke softly, close to her ear, and his words gave her courage. "You have so much power. When you run, even the wind can't catch you."

"I'll get through that hole."

"I know you will."

"I'll get help."

His sad smile seemed to say that he was beyond help. "I meant everything I've said these past few days. Everything. Except the obnoxious stuff."

"Don't make any promises or declarations. Let's wait and see what happens when we wake up."

"What do you mean?"

"Let's wait and see how things turn out when this nightmare is finally over."

"I couldn't have survived this long without you."

"You still might not, if I don't get a move on. You said so yourself."

"Be careful," he implored.

"I will."

"I'll see you when we wake up."

She climbed onto the tub and grabbed the sides of the hole. "Reece?"

She looked back at him.

Sunlight caught in his eyes, and they sparkled like jewels. "I never really minded you calling me Chris."

Chapter Fifteen

She got through.

She didn't make a sound when the sharp edges of the tin border caught her skin and tore it despite the lubrication provided by the sunscreen, and she kept quiet when that troublesome nail head gouged a seven-inch gash in her right thigh. Silently she twisted, contorted and compressed herself until she was practically dangling from the hole by her feet.

She let herself fall to the hard-packed dirt below, landing on her hands and rolling with her weight as her body fell after her. Taryn had taught her more than punches and kicks. She had also taught her how to fall.

She sat on the ground, rubbing the most offended parts of her anatomy. She was thankful for the fact that large breasts skipped every other Wyndham girl. Bailey and Mallory were following in Taryn's 36C bra straps. Reece and Kelsey topped out at 32A, for once a blessing.

Reece had never minded her breast size as much as the boys who ogled her seemed to, because her legs were her favorite feature. She had her mother's legs. They were long and well-muscled without being sinewy or bulky. What she liked most about them was their strength.

Christopher dropped her T-shirt and shoes out after her, and she slipped the filthy things back on. She anxiously waited for her jeans to come down so she could put her shoes on. The longer he took, the more worried she became.

She wondered if he had passed out and was lying unconscious on the cold, dirty tile. She was scanning the ground for a pebble to toss up at the window when a piece of denim dropped out of the sky. She held it up. He had ripped her jeans into shorts.

She quickly pulled them on, laced on her running shoes, and crept alongside the house. Ducking into the cornfield, she made her way to the road and stepped onto the blacktop. In either direction, as far as she could see, there was only the two-lane road.

Every car they had heard in the past few days had come from the east, so without a look back, Reece ran into the sunrise.

He would have replaced the vent cover if he could have hauled himself onto the tub once more, but with the last of his strength, Christopher lowered himself to the floor. He brought one of the amputated legs of Reece's jeans to his cheek. He lay in a puddle of the early morning light and closed his eyes.

Reece was a sprinter, but she adjusted to become a long-distance runner. She ran evenly, steadily, powerfully and fast, as though the gates of hell had opened behind her and released its fiercest demons. There was nothing but asphalt before her, sky above her, and ripening corn on either side of the road.

She was mindless of the sun beating upon her and the dryness of her mouth. The burning in her thighs and calves didn't distract her from the task of putting one foot before the other in long, graceful strides.

She was lost in the methodical rhythm of her footsteps and her breathing. She could have run forever if she had to, as she worked muscles that had been knotted in fear for four days. She might have run all the way to St. Louis if she hadn't seen a dusty, roadside station called Drake's Fill & Go. The tiny building was unremarkable except for the fact that it was across the street from a place called Dixie's Luncheonette.

The hillbilly nightmare continues, Reece thought as the door to Dixie's swung shut behind her. The place was tiny. There were four booths along a wall opposite six stools at a marbled linoleum counter. A stocky, short-order cook stood between the counter and the grill. He wielded a wide metal spatula in a chubby, floured fist. A plump waitress in a lemon yellow uniform noisily chatted with the diners at the counter. Her hair was in a tall beehive immobilized behind a nylon hairnet.

She served a plate of steaming flapjacks to a man on a stool. He was so big the stool seemed to bow beneath him, and his haunches hung like saddlebags over the marbleized vinyl of the seat. A second waitress, a younger woman wearing bright red lipstick and a lip ring, took breakfast orders from customers in a booth.

The big man at the counter was the only person who didn't turn to stare when Reece said, "I need a phone."

"You look like you been rollin' with a badger," the beehived waitress said, snapping her gum. She pointed to the far end of the counter near the plate glass window. "Pay phone's over yonder."

The big muscles of Reece's thighs quivered and convulsed as she placed a hand on the counter for support. She shook her head to clear it of dizziness and nausea.

"Somethin' ain't right with that one," the beehive told the cook as she suspiciously eyed Reece. "I ain't never seen 'er 'round here b'for."

The younger waitress appeared behind Reece. "You need some help, darlin'?"

"Yes!" Reece yelled over a sob. "I need the police, and a doctor for Christopher, and my parents, and...get out of my way!"

The waitress stepped back. Every eye was on Reece as she grabbed the phone, sobbing. She raised her hand to dial 911 when she noticed the OUT OF ORDER sign posted over it. With a cry of frustration she pounded the receiver back into the cradle.

"I need a phone!" she screamed at the people in the luncheonette. "Why are you all just sitting there? Don't any of you have cell phones? Call the police!"

Her left hamstrings cramped and she crumbled to the floor. The big man at the counter very calmly eased his bulk off of the stool. If there had been anything in her bladder, Reece would have wet herself as he lumbered toward her.

It was early in the morning, but sweat stains darkened the

armpits of his plaid shirt. His stomach lopped over his belt and he was as broad as a garage door.

Reece was too scared to scream, to move, to even breath as the biggest Liggett of them all came at her. The big man squatted in front of her, a safe distance from the long lengths of her lethal-looking legs.

His resemblance to the Liggets stopped at his eyes. They were a very light shade of brown flecked with black and gold. They were kind, and Reece's fear left with her next exhalation.

"You look like you just run out of a horror flick, gal," he said.

"Sweet Baby Jesus!" cried the younger waitress. "I knew it was you!" She ran up to Reece, smiling wide. "I was up to St. Louis yesterday, visitin' my sister in Dogtown," she told the big man, "and this gal was on tv." She waved the older waitress over. "Get the paper! It's on the gossip pages. This is the gal who ran away with that rich boy."

"We were kidnapped," Reece said in a clear, strong voice meant to penetrate the forebrain of even the most feeble-minded hillbilly-goth waitress. "Call the police."

"Which way you come from?" the big man asked.

Reece pointed west.

The big man gave her another look. "How long you been runnin'?"

"I don't know. I escaped a little after sunrise, when that siren went off."

"Ain't nothin' out that way for near 'bout twenty miles." The big man started back to his plate of fried ham, bacon, biscuits, scrambled eggs and flapjacks. "I ain't about to waste a good breakfast. When you want to tell me the truth, I'll listen."

"Listen to me now, you jackass!" Reece shouted through angry tears. "We were kept in an old yellow house with boarded windows! Christopher is still there. He's hurt really badly. Please, someone, call the police. Please, help me! They might have killed him already because I got away." Her voice broke and she angrily wiped her eyes. "Ross and Gentry Liggett took us there. Lester Oliver planned the whole thing."

The big man turned back to Reece, his eyes flickering with interest and something more dangerous. The old Liggett place was a good eighteen miles away. The siren at the old auto plant had gone off less than two hours ago. "You must run pretty fast, gal," he said.

"When I run," she sobbed, "even the wind can't catch me. I hope I ran fast enough."

The man looked over his shoulder and said, "Wyatt, Early, let's ride on out the Liggett place and get us a look 'round."

"You should wait for the police," Reece told him, clutching his arm. "The Liggetts have guns."

The big man smiled lazily but his eyes remained hard and determined. He patted the bulge at his right hip. "So do we."

Juniper Falls had two major roads. The big man sent his brother Early and one of the other men to Juniper Lane, which was also known as Rural Route 6 and flanked the west side of the old Liggett farm. The big man went back the way Reece had come, along Route 33, the road that led to the house. He picked up his CB radio and put in a call to the Juniper Falls police station, which also served as the fire department and town hall.

"This is Sheriff Judd Tatum out Route 33," he began. "I think I got that huckleberry missing from St. Louis out at the old Liggett place. Requesting immediate back up. And send the cruiser to Dixie's to take a patient to Doc Soames. I got a young girl there in need of emergency medical attention. Repeat, Sheriff Tatum requesting immediate back up at the Liggett farm, over."

Armed with a semi-automatic 9mm and a cell phone, Gentry burst into the empty room. He violently flinched as gunshots were fired downstairs. He hit the speed dial button that would ring Lester's office number at Daley International, Inc.

"Answer, Les," he whined as he went to the bathroom to

get Christopher and Reece.

Christopher lay on the floor. Ross hollered at the sheriff and deputies downstairs, his words broken by gunshots. Gentry jumped at a loud gun blast shattering through a downstairs room, and Oliver finally answered the phone.

"Lester!" Gentry cried. "Sheriff Tatum is here. Ross fired at 'em. They's all shootin' up the place. They done found us out, an' Miss Reece is gone!"

Terrified and perplexed, Gentry knew Reece hadn't lapsed into a coma or died. There hadn't been enough knock-out drops to fill the syringe after he'd accidentally broken the last full vial Oliver had given them. Gentry had used the last of the first vial, and then made up the difference with water rather than risk incurring Oliver's wrath. He'd thought that there was enough of the drug in the syringe to put Reece to sleep, not transport her right on up to heaven.

A rifle blast rocked the house. Ross's outraged shouting and cursing abruptly ceased. Soon after, heavy footsteps thundered up the stairs.

"They's comin', Les, what am I s'posed to do?"

"You're on your own, Gentry," Oliver responded calmly before hanging up.

Gentry tossed the dead phone aside. "I ain't gone' die 'cause 'a you!" he screamed at Christopher, gripping the gun in both hands and aiming it at his head. "You stay right there!" he yelled. "You're my hostage 'n don't you even try to run!"

Christopher was in no condition to run. He was in no condition to stand.

The footsteps breached the empty room where Christopher and Reece had been held captive. "Give yourself up, Gentry!" Sheriff Tatum yelled. "I ain't gonna tell you twice!"

Sheriff Tatum and one of his deputies moved into the bathroom doorway. He fixed Gentry in the sights of his rifle. "Drop it, Gentry."

"I'm leavin' 'n I'm takin' my hostage with me, so don't you try nothin', Sheriff, or I'll blow his brains all over this tile!" He put the gun to Christopher's temple.

His weapon still on Gentry, the sheriff stole a peek at Christopher. "You ain't gonna get far with that huckleberry slowin' you down, Gentry. He's bad off. You wanna add a murder charge to kidnapping?"

"Ross!" Gentry cried wildly. "Ross, where are you?"

"He can't answer you, son," the sheriff said. "Ross Liggett is finally done tellin' you what to do."

It took a long, tense moment for the information to sink in, but once it did, Gentry seemed to calm.

"Which one 'a y'all done it?" he asked. "Who shot my brother?"

"Ross shot at me first, Gentry," said the sheriff. "I responded in kind."

Gentry saw the bloody wound in Sheriff Tatum's shoulder. "Is he dead, truly?"

"I'm sorry, Gentry."

The 9mm was still pressed to Christopher's head. Gentry muttered under his breath, debating with himself, and then pulled the trigger.

So did Sheriff Tatum.

Oliver stared out the window of his office. He hyperventilated as the gun blasts in Juniper Falls echoed in his head. Ross and Gentry had been discovered. He was next.

He slammed his fists on his desktop. What had gone so wrong? Everything had turned out well last night. The morning papers had called the kidnapping a hoax, with the exception of the *St. Louis News-Chronicle*. Katy Odenkirk had run an exclusive interview with Stirling Barton in spite of Augie Daley's insistence that Christopher was out of town. The Wyndhams had claimed that Reece was in Baltimore, on a campus visit to Johns Hopkins University. Katy had also offered the absurd possibility that Christopher and Reece had run away together on a Romeo and Juliet-like romantic escapade.

The media coverage could not have worked out better, because the whole of St. Louis seemed to be laughing at Stirling and Katy.

Oliver wasn't laughing, not now. He opened his desk drawer and put his hands on his car keys, frantically wondering how long he had—two minutes? ten?—before the authorities came for him. Even if he made it to the parking garage before the crackerjack Janus security force apprehended him, what then? Was there any place he could go where Augie Daley wouldn't find him? Where could he hide with no money?

What had Gentry meant when he said that Reece was gone? He'd never know.

The Pulse One stun gun sat beside his car keys. Lester "Leighton" Oliver put the device on its highest setting and applied it directly to his chest, left of center.

Christopher kept his gaze on Reece. He had no memory of events beyond the empty click of the gun at his head, and he thought that was probably a good thing, considering the tremendous amount of pain raging through his body. He'd opened his eyes to find himself floating high in the sky, the roar of a helicopter's engine drowning out the voices around him and Reece. She lay on a gurney flush against his, her tangle of wires and tubing indistinguishable from his.

Blood smeared her cheek, her lower lip trembled. He tried to smile, to let her know how proud he was of her. But either his face refused to cooperate, or she failed to see him through her half-lidded eyes. Someone worked at the needle at the crook of his elbow, and a peculiar heaviness assaulted his senses.

He struggled to keep his eyes open, fighting the sudden weight of his eyelids. He needed to see Reece. She had so much strength. With her near and in sight, he could hold on, second by second, until he could thank her for saving his life.

Chapter Sixteen

"Thank you, for seeing me today." Mrs. Daley seated herself at the chef's isle in the center of Mrs. Wyndham's Home Sciences Resources room.

"I teach here," Mrs. Wyndham said. "You're a parent. It shouldn't arouse suspicion for us to be speaking with each other."

Mrs. Daley gazed into her coffee mug. "I want to apologize, for what Augie's done over the past few weeks."

The Wyndhams and the Daleys had last seen each other in Juniper Falls, Missouri, when they'd brought their children home. Not one to waste time or mince words, Mr. Daley had chosen that emotionally-wrenching moment to ask the Wyndhams what it would cost to buy their silence regarding what had come to be known as 'the incident.'

"I will not have every money-hungry maniac between the Atlantic and the Pacific stalking my family, and that's exactly what would happen if the truth gets out," Mr. Daley had ranted during the helicopter ride to Juniper Falls. "Nicole, Christopher and I will deny any story that you, your wife, or your daughter gives to the press."

"Augie, you're being unreasonable," Mrs. Daley had protested.

"Is that the 'truth' you're afraid of, Daley?" Mr. Wyndham had countered furiously. "Or is it that you're afraid people will find out that not even a billionaire can protect his family?"

The worst, though, had been Mr. Daley's decree ordering Christopher and Reece to return to "life as usual," meaning they should maintain the same relationship they had prior to the kidnapping. He wanted nothing to lend credence to the rumors that refused to die thanks to Katy Odenkirk's tenacious snooping.

Katy had attended the funeral of the man they knew as Leighton Oliver, hoping to find something to connect his suicide at the Janus to the kidnapping.

"I wanted you to know that I don't agree with Augie," Mrs.

Daley told Mrs. Wyndham on a golden October afternoon. "I don't think we should keep our children separated."

"That's kind of you to say, but it's been over a month now," said Mrs. Wyndham. "It hasn't been easy for Reece. She didn't sleep her first week back home, and then the nightmares started. She slept in my bed for five nights."

"Forgive me, Sara, but isn't Reece a little old to be sharing a bed with you and your husband?"

"Craig has been sleeping on the sofa since the incident." Mrs. Wyndham dropped her eyes. "This has been very difficult for him. When he saw Reece in Juniper Falls—it broke his heart." *And his spirit,* Mrs. Wyndham thought on a long sigh.

Mrs. Daley closed her eyes and saw Reece, her elegant, athletic body covered in road grime and blood, draped over her father's lap as he wheeled her to the rescue helicopter.

That picture was followed by the heartbreaking image of her own child, his skin colorless except for bruises, burns, cuts and blood, his eyes preternaturally bright from the infection raging through his body.

"I'm sorry," Mrs. Wyndham said sincerely as if she'd read the other woman's thoughts. She placed her hand over Mrs. Daley's.

The simple gesture bolstered Mrs. Daley. "Just as Augie wanted, I've stuck religiously to my normal routine. I go to the club, I go to the office, I lunch at The Rise with a gaggle of women with whom I've discovered I no longer have anything in common. I'm different now. Even if I told everyone what really happened, you're the only person who can truly understand."

"Is that why you're here?"

Mrs. Daley gave her a guilty smile.

"How is Christopher?" Mrs. Wyndham asked. "Every time Reece calls, a woman answers and tells her that he's unavailable. She makes it sound as though he's out playing golf."

"That would be Hilda, Christopher's nurse," Mrs. Daley said bitterly. "She's Darth Vader in orthopedic shoes. She hardly lets *me* near Christopher." She nervously tapped the side of her Kate Spade handbag, desperately wanting to light up a Galois.

Mrs. Wyndham picked up the coffee mugs and motioned for Mrs. Daley to follow her through a wall of sliding glass doors. They went to the shady grove of Japanese maples in back of the Home Sciences room, where a weathered wooden bench was centered beneath the canopies of the trees.

Mrs. Daley drew a slim cigarette from a gold case in her purse, and she pinched it between her lips. Her hands shook as she lit it with a monogrammed lighter. "Physically, Christopher is so much better. When we got to him in Juniper Falls, he'd suffered a tear in his left kidney. The doctor said it was caused by blunt force trauma. During his captivity, the site became infected, and the infection spread. He lost the kidney.

"Remember Randolph Soames, the doctor who treated the kids in Juniper Falls?" She took a nervous puff of her cigarette. "He was chief of surgery at Boston General Medical Center for twelve years. He said he left New England to practice in his hometown for two reasons. One, 'because hillbillies need doctors same as everybody else,' and two, because he 'got tired of ladling out brimming bowls of bureaucratic bull.' I like his style."

"I'm glad he was there when our children needed him," said Mrs. Wyndham.

"We flew in a specialist to repair Christopher's scars and yesterday he was fitted for a false tooth. He's coming back to school tomorrow. Frankly, I was amazed when Mr. Edwards told me that Reece was back at school a week after the rescue."

"The hospital kept her for two days," Mrs. Wyndham said. "Her physical injuries weren't severe. Christopher took good care of her. He protected her." Mrs. Wyndham scuffed the toes of her beige espadrilles in the grass. "Craig was furious when your husband paid Reece's medical bills."

Mrs. Daley exhaled a long breath of smoke. "That's the least Augie could do after Reece saved Christopher's life. Augie donated the ransom money to the town of Juniper Falls. In exchange for signed writs of confidentiality from the townspeople involved in the incident, Augie established a ten-million dollar development fund to be administered by Sheriff

Tatum and Dr. Soames. They plan to build a new high school and a trade school to teach computer and business skills to the people who lost their jobs when the auto plant closed. Things seem to be working out well for everyone." She ground out her cigarette. "Life goes on. Augie pretends that nothing happened. That's not so easy for me."

"Or Christopher."

"Would it be too much to ask, for us to be friends, Sara?"

"If I remember correctly that would be the opposite of what your husband wants us to do."

"What my husband wants and what his wife and child need are two entirely different things."

"I could use a friend, Nicole." Mrs. Wyndham dropped her eyes to her lap, where her right hand anxiously twisted the gold band on her left hand.

"So could Christopher," Mrs. Daley said. "He called a psychiatrist, a woman named Carol Livingston. Her son is in Christopher's English class. Hilda intercepted Dr. Livingston's return call and reported it to Augie. He became livid and told Christopher to toughen up and get on with his life. Christopher needs to talk about this with someone who can help him. Reece is the only one who knows what he suffered."

"Reece will be here tomorrow," Mrs. Wyndham said.

"Don't be surprised if you look out of your classroom and see an ex-Green Beret here, too. Augie's paid for extra security at Prescott. Mr. Edwards, the headmaster, is the only person outside our circle who knows the truth of what happened to Christopher and Reece."

"I think the students might notice armed guards outside their classrooms," Mrs. Wyndham said skeptically.

"Not if they're pruning the box hedges and masquerading as maintenance men," Mrs. Daley said.

Everyone watched Christopher as he entered the lobby of McWhorter Auditorium. This was his first day at school after a five-week absence. Conversations quieted, but none of his classmates greeted him as he entered the senior lounge.

There were plenty of empty seats. The plush, cushioned chairs flanking the stereo system and the leather sofa at one end of the lounge were unoccupied. He went to the matching sofa at the opposite end of the lounge, where Reece sat with her toes propped on the edge of a low table. She was reading from a history textbook opened across her knees.

Christopher sat beside her. He put his feet up on the table, his leather upper an inch from the canvas of her sneaker.

Like the rest of the seniors, Reece looked at him. He wore a heavy cable knit sweater with a high rolled collar, and a pair of wide-wale corduroy trousers the color of oatmeal. The sweater was the same deep blue as his eyes. His dark, wavy hair was a little longer than usual, but the look suited him.

He looked really good. She was about to tell him when he spoke over her. "Could I borrow your notes for *The Sound and the Fury*? I've missed some American Literature classes and I have a lot of catching up to do."

Disappointed, she nodded. *He's going to play his father's little game after all,* she thought despondently. She picked up her English notebook and thrust it at him. He leafed through the pages, looking for the notes.

The other seniors watched the exchange with more than a little interest, but they saw no outward signs of anything interesting between Reece and Christopher, so they went back to their own business. No one saw Reece smile when Christopher slid his hand down to the seat and linked his littlest finger with hers.

Chapter Seventeen

"We have to stop meeting like this." Christopher stepped out of the Home Sciences Resource Room and into the shade of the Japanese maples where Reece sat on the bench studying a collection of photographs for an upcoming Art Appreciation exam.

"We can't. This is the only place on campus where we can be alone without being stared at."

Their sanctuary was wedged between the dining hall wing of the main building and the athletic complex. A tall, thick box hedge and a fence concealed it from the rear driveway of the campus, as well as a huge maintenance shed. The only access to the cozy area was through Mrs. Wyndham's classroom, and when Reece and Christopher were out there, Mrs. Wyndham guarded the sliding doors like a lioness at the mouth of her den.

In the two weeks since Christopher's return to school, they hadn't been disturbed by anyone other than Mrs. Wyndham, who ventured out just long enough to bring icy mugs of milk and freshly-baked cookies. Christopher practically lived on Mrs. Wyndham's oatmeal raisin cookies.

"Your mom looks a little sad today." Christopher joined Reece on the bench. He sat as she did, with his back to the opposite armrest and his feet in the middle of the seat. He brought his feet forward until the tips of his Cole Haans touched the toes of her Nikes. "So do you."

The Japanese maples were at the height of their fall color. Reece reached up and plucked one of the glossy maroon leaves from an overhanging branch. She used it to mark her page before closing the book. "My parents had another fight last night."

"About us?" Christopher asked. Reece's eyes were so large and dark. He had no trouble reading her emotions in them.

She shook her head. The one thing their fathers agreed on was that Reece and Christopher shouldn't see each other. Augie didn't want anyone to know the truth. Craig didn't want Reece to be in danger ever again.

"Daddy's given up trying to stop me from seeing you. He can't fight me and mom together." She sighed. "He's so angry at her, all the time now. He never even looks at her anymore."

Christopher peered through the sliding doors. Mrs. Wyndham sat at the counter that doubled as her desk. Her head was bowed over a lesson plan. Her black hair was held back with a white headband embroidered with tiny whales. She wore a pink oxford, navy chinos, and Nikes just like Reece's. She was so pretty and energetic. She didn't look old enough to be the mother of six practically grown-up children. "Your dad doesn't know when he's got something good, does he?"

"He's throwing it away with both hands."

"What was the fight about?"

"Mom thought they should get away together, just the two of them, for a weekend. Daddy refused. Taryn's moved back home and I told him that I'd be fine, but he won't listen to anyone."

"You and your sisters are welcome to stay at my house," he offered. "The place is as secure as the Federal Reserve now."

"Thanks, but…"

"But your dad hates me."

"It's not you. He doesn't like your father. He doesn't like feeling helpless. When your dad paid my hospital bills without asking, Dad nearly—"

"He did that?"

"You didn't know?"

"My father hasn't spoken to me about any of it," Christopher said. "After I was released from the hospital I tried to talk to him about that school in England he wanted to send me to."

She swung her legs to the ground and moved closer to him. "You're leaving?"

He put his right foot on the ground and she moved into the crook of his legs. "I thought about it." He put his arms around her. She rested her head on his chest, and his breath lightly brushed her hair when he said, "I thought it would be best if I got away from here. My father was sizzling to send me away last year. Now he says I have to stay and keep up appearances. I suppose that's what *he* did, by telling everyone that I was gone for so long because I was injured in a water-skiing accident on the Cape. He won't face it. Every time I try to talk to him, to tell him what they did to me…"

His hands shook, no matter how tightly Reece held them.

"My father's friends and business associates sent flowers and cards, wishing me a speedy recovery from my made-up accident. Only two people from school tried to find out how I was."

She knew she was one of them. "Who was the other one?"

"Crystal Henry brought me a quart of daiquiri ice from Baskin-Robbins. I don't know how she knew it, but daiquiri ice is my favorite. She brought it on the day my dad said I had to tough it out here at Prescott. That was my lowest moment. I was so sore and so sick of being sick and alone. I wanted some ice cream, and all we had in the house was that imported stuff my mother flies in from Italy once a month. Two minutes later, Bigelow came up to my room with the daiquiri ice and a spoon. He said a schoolmate came by and dropped it off. He offered to sneak her in past Hilda, but the girl refused to come in. She wouldn't even give him her name. When he described her, I knew it was Crystal Henry. I was disappointed, but only because she wasn't you."

"Crystal Henry? I didn't know you guys were friends. I didn't know Crystal had any friends at all."

"We aren't, not really. I took a creative writing seminar at Riverside Community College over the summer. I didn't think I'd run into anybody from Prescott at a junior college, but Crystal was in the same class. She's a very good writer. Since we were the youngest people in the class, we were paired to critique each other's stories."

"She's really a disaster. She used to tell everybody that her father was a fighter pilot in the Air Force and that he lived in Hawaii."

"Sometimes a lie is the only thing that keeps the truth from killing you," Christopher said. "My dad is living proof."

Chapter Eighteen

Prescott divided itself into three camps: those who believed the false stories about Christopher and Reece, those who didn't, and those who didn't care one way or the other.

Big, blond, Larry Odenkirk was the self-appointed commander-in-chief of the first camp. His best friends, Dan McNamara and Michael Littlefield, belonged to the second and third, respectively.

The three boys sat in the senior lounge, munching on french fries and onion rings. Michael was a prefect and had the privilege of leaving campus for lunch one day a week. He had picked up some grub for Dan, a junior, and Larry, who didn't have the grades to be a prefect.

Dan could be in the senior lounge with impunity only because he was with Larry and Michael.

"My sister got it straight from Reece's brother-in-law." Larry shoved a fistful of fries into his mouth and chewed them as he spoke. "Reece wasn't in Baltimore visiting a college like everyone said. Katy's got all kinds of contacts in New York. If Reece had been in Baltimore, Katy would have been able to find someone who could verify she was there."

"Baltimore is in Maryland, dink." Dan laughed around a mouthful of cheeseburger.

"Kiss my Maryland, dude," said Larry.

"Get over it, Larry," Dan said. "Nobody's been able to find any proof to back up Stirling's story."

"That's because Daley fixed it!" Larry declared vehemently. "Katy got a call from a nurse at St. Mary's. Christopher had burns."

"He was in a boating accident," Dan said. "You can get burned in boating accidents."

"They were cigar burns," Larry insisted.

"You're so full of it," Michael snorted.

Dan wickedly tweaked Larry further. "Even Stirling didn't have proof. He was on channel 25 saying there was a ransom video, but he couldn't prove it."

"Why would someone kidnap Reece?" Michael asked. He wiped his greasy hands on the leg of his pleated trousers.

Larry grinned lasciviously. "I've thought about kidnapping her myself." He slapped a high five with Michael. "Maybe the kidnappers wanted to mix business with pleasure."

"If the story is true, then why was Katy suspended from the *Chronicle*?" Dan asked. He flinched, expecting a punch for pushing Larry's buttons one time too many. Larry was as protective as a Rottweiler when it came to his big sister.

Larry kept his big fists to himself. "If it's *not* true, then why did KYNN fire Stirling?"

"Because he lied on air and almost started a national panic." Dan slurped up the last of his chocolate shake.

"He was the best sports guy in town," Michael said. "I'm gonna miss his Dumb Jock of the Week bloopers."

"Stirling was fired because the story is true and he wouldn't keep quiet," Larry persisted. "Christopher was kidnapped."

The bell rang and Larry lumbered off to his eighth period class.

"Tomorrow is Halloween," Dan said mischievously. "If Larry wants a kidnapping so bad, let's give him one."

Michael's ears perked up beneath his bright cap of red hair. "What do you have in mind?"

Felix Nayland wore yellow pants, a yellow turtleneck, and a pair of bright yellow Hush Puppies. His hair, face and hands were yellow, and his whole body was covered in diagonal black stripes. Felix was Cliff's Notes, the bane of the Prescott English department. Students found with Cliff's Notes in their possession received an automatic F in whatever English class they were taking.

Naturally, Felix's costume was a huge hit.

"Okay," Felix said, reading the note attached to the screen of the big screen television in the corner of the senior lounge. "Insert disc A," he held up the CD, "into slot B." The mouth of the VCR was marked with a Post-It printed with a big letter B.

Felix followed the simple instructions and turned on the television.

Seniors dressed as X-Men and Avatar characters, a bunch of grapes and green M&Ms, ballerinas and saloon girls, and assorted cows, pigs, bulldogs and cats, crowded in front of the television. Christopher lingered on the fringe of the group, dressed only as himself in blue jeans and a Shetland sweater over a Lacoste shirt.

Every costumed character laughed when Larry Odenkirk appeared onscreen wearing red-and-yellow striped boxers and white tube socks. He was sitting in a chair, blindfolded, his hands bound behind him. His ankles were tied with thick, white rope. "C'mon guys!" he yelled. "This isn't funny, okay? Gag's over, okay?"

Some of the seniors laughed while others looked at each other in uncomfortable uncertainty. The tape ended, and Felix read the second note.

"If you ever want to see Larry again, the following demands must be met. Deliver the following items to the stone planter in back of Schaeffer Library by assembly, or Larry will get it." Felix shuddered dramatically before he read the ransom items. "One copy of the new Karmic Echo CD, a bottle of Super Fruity Ultra-Shine lip gloss, a pair of satin panties, a black bra, a box of wooden matches from Under the Bridge, two pounds of Swedish Fish, a lock of Logan Maddox's hair, and twenty dollars in loose change."

A few senior girls enthusiastically set about collecting as much of Larry's ransom as they could before the bell rang for morning assembly.

Chrissie Abernathy, who was dressed up as the *Like A Virgin*-era Madonna, donated the lip gloss. Betsy Pruett-Fogharty, dressed as a nun, contributed the bra and panties. Megan Finer and Leslie Kincaid gathered girls to find the Karmic Echo CD. Russ Taggart went to the school store for the Swedish Fish, and Caroline Moss, armed with a tiny pair of manicure scissors, hunted for Logan Maddox.

An empty tennis ball canister set on a table served as the collection container for the Save Larry Loose Change fund.

"I saw Christopher Daley in the library yesterday listening to the new Karmic Echo on his iPod," Lucy Fischel said as she looked around the lounge. She was dressed as 'Columbia' from *The Rocky Horror Picture Show*. "He was sitting on the sofa a minute ago. Figures he'd run off when you need something from him."

The bell for assembly rang.

Christopher was behind the Home Sciences Resource Room, his hands clamped over his ears. The sound of the bell went on and on, filling his head, bombarding his whole body with noise.

Just like the siren in Juniper Falls.

He wrapped his arms around his head and pulled his feet up to the seat of the bench. Even after the bell had shut up the echo of it continued to resonate through his body, stopping his breath and clogging his chest with fear and panic.

The Home Sciences room was dark. Mrs. Wyndham had taken Reece to an 8 o'clock doctor's appointment for a follow-up on her leg. They should have been at school by now. Why weren't they back?

"Where are you?" he whimpered. He rocked back and forth on his heels, his hands covering his ears, his eyes shut tight. He couldn't stop trembling or erase Juniper Falls from his mind, and tears wet the knees of his of his jeans. "I need you, Reece," he moaned. "I need you."

Three large GAP shopping bags filled with clothing arrived first, followed by two big bags of shoes, boots and accessories from the Timberland store. A box of movies, music and exercise DVDs from Parliament Entertainment was brought in next, followed by CDs from MusicWorld, lushly scented bath and relaxation products from The Body Shop, boxes and bags of candy from The Sweet Factory and Godiva Chocolatiers, delicately wrapped boxes from Victoria's Secret, and clothing from Banana Republic, Abercrombie & Fitch, Talbot's and The Warner Brothers Studio Store. Somehow, the deliverymen squeezed everything into the tiny living room of the Wyndham house.

The assistant manager of the Nordic Track store at the Galleria Mall delivered the treadmill, which he had to leave on the rear deck because it was too wide to fit into the bulkhead leading into the basement.

The owner of Seymour Fowler Jewelers and two security guards hand-delivered a white velvet case and stood by as the Wyndham women watched Reece open it. On a bed of snowy white satin rested a platinum choker. White diamonds surrounded a flawless chocolate sapphire that perfectly matched Reece's eyes.

"Uh, Reece?" Kelsey twirled the end of one of the scarves she was wearing as part of her belly dancer costume. "Maybe you should give Richie Rich a call and tell him that it's Halloween, not Christmas."

Reece snapped the jewelry box shut and stepped over boxes and bags to get to the phone in the kitchen. Mr. Wyndham was already in there. He had come in from the deck, where he spent most of his time, for a cup of coffee.

With her father glaring at her, Reece dialed Christopher's private number. She let it ring twelve times, then hung up and tried again.

"All of it goes back," Mr. Wyndham grunted as he wheeled himself back out onto the deck.

Kelsey stuck her head into the kitchen. "There's another delivery for you, Reece," she crooned. "This one walked in on its own."

Chapter Nineteen

Mr. Wyndham sat on the patio while his wife and daughters sorted through the mountain of packages that had been delivered from the Galleria Mall. "Maybe Christopher didn't send this stuff," Kelsey suggested. She danced with her scarves around a knee-high pyramid of shoeboxes.

"Sure," Bailey said skeptically. "Reece just won every *Teen Vogue* contest she ever entered."

Taryn held up a black Calvin Klein dress. "Everything is in your size, Reece. This dress would look great on you. Christopher's got a good eye. And great taste."

"I'm not keeping any of this." Reece inched her way around a pyramid of boxed gifts to get to the stairs.

"Not even Bono?" Mallory protested, horrified. In less than an hour she had named and fallen in love with an eight-month-old bundle of ropy black hair, the Hungarian Sheepdog puppy lightly snoring in Kyle's lap.

"Can I have these?" Kelsey fell out of a pirouette to grab a pair of Timberland hiking boots.

"No," Reece said sharply. "Everything goes back in the morning." She took the stairs in twos as she ran up to her room to try Christopher's number one last time.

He still didn't answer.

On a sudden inspiration, she dialed his car phone. He answered on the first ring.

"I went overboard," he said by way of greeting.

She chuckled in spite of herself. "Yeah, you kinda did. Chris, this is crazy."

"I think I am crazy."

"What? I can hardly hear you. There's static on the line."

"I said I'm crazy about you."

She fell back onto her bunk bed, smiling. "If this is how you celebrate Halloween, will I need my own warehouse for Christmas?"

"I wanted you to know how much you mean to me," he said. The line suddenly cleared.

She ran her finger along a green stripe on her plaid comforter. "Presents don't show me how much you care about me. Your words do. I can't keep those gifts. They cost way too much. That choker doesn't even look real."

"Then Seymour Fowler has a lot of explaining to do."

"That's not what I mean. That necklace looks like it should be in the Smithsonian, not around my neck."

"We can take it back and get something else, if you want."

"You're deliberately missing the point." She bounced off of her bed and paced the small room she and Bailey were once again sharing with Taryn. "I can't keep those things. It's not just because we don't have room for them. That treadmill is half the size of our living room! You should have seen my Dad's face when the delivery guys put it on the deck."

"You aren't running. I thought you might like it, so you can exercise at home."

She stood by the window. "I haven't felt like running."

"You don't have to explain."

"The treadmill has to go back," she said quietly. "So do the clothes and the shoes and the movies—"

"You're sending Prince Erno back, too?"

"Yes, the perfume goes back, too."

"Prince Erno is the puppy," Christopher explained. "He's pedigreed."

"Kyle and Mallory are spoiling him to death. His name is Bono now."

"Bono?"

"Wyndham girls dig U2."

"I hope you keep the dog."

"I might not have much choice. If I try to get rid of him, Mallory and Kyle just might go along with him. Chris?"

"Yes?"

"Are you still driving?"

"I parked so I could talk to you."

"Where are you?"

"Behind you."

She turned and pulled back the curtains closed over the

window. A black BMW roadster was parked at the curb in front of her front door.

"Where are your bodyguards?" she asked as she got into the car and closed the door.

Christopher activated the automatic locks. "I ditched them at the mall. It was easy, once I threw a handful of tokens into the air at the arcade and slipped into a mob of 13-year-olds."

"I heard about what Michael and Dan did to Larry at school today. Did you leave early because of that, or because you needed a little time to shop?"

He stared at his hands, which sat in his lap like injured birds. "It was the video. Larry was so scared. Even though it was a joke, he was so scared. They snatched him from his house at six this morning. They kept him tied up for three hours."

She held his hand. Three hours in the heated, furnished, carpeted boys dressing room above the drama teacher's office was cake compared to what Christopher had endured.

"It was a joke, Chris." She rested their clasped hands on her bare thigh. "Larry didn't seem any the worse for wear."

She wore shorts and an oversized T-shirt, her typical sitting-around-the-house outfit. He was wearing the same clothes he'd worn to school.

"That's what was so hard," he said. "Everyone thinks it's all a joke. What happened to us wasn't a joke. I couldn't stay at school, but I was too scared to go home.

"My father opens the house every year, to the kids from the Rosa Hicks Homeless Shelter. The north garden gets turned into a Haunted Hayride and the tennis courts are set up with carnival games. The parents get to hang out in the ballroom, knowing that their children are safe from the real hobgoblins and trolls.

"I couldn't go home." Misery welled in his chest. "All of those strangers, right there in the house. I was scared to be in my own home."

"So you went to the mall."

He nodded and chuckled sadly. "It seemed safer. I mean,

who's going to grab me at a mall with ten thousand little Trick or Treaters and their parents watching."

She leaned across the seat and hugged him. "Thank you, for all of the presents. I know a lot of thought went into each one."

He buried his face in her neck as he hugged her, hoping that if he held her tight enough, it would last him through the night. "Promise me you'll keep Prince Erno. I mean, Bono."

"I promise."

"And that you'll keep this." He let go of her to reach into the backseat for the one gift he had wanted to give her himself. He pressed it into her hand. She moved into his arms again, careful not to bend or bruise the perfect, fresh daisy he had given her.

Chapter Twenty

Decorators had spent three weeks working full-time to prepare Daley Manor for the Christmas holiday season. When the huddled Wyndham girls entered the banquet hall, they were overwhelmed by the majesty of the place.

"It's beautiful," Mrs. Wyndham said, her head tilted back to gazed at a fifteen-tier crystal chandelier adorned with miniature poinsettias and snow lilies. The mansion had been transformed into a wintry, fairy tale palace.

"Mom, it's better than beautful!" Kelsey exclaimed. She twirled in circles in the dining room, her glossy, chestnut hair fanning out as she performed an impromptu dance around the long dining table. "I feel like a princess."

"Kelsey, that's enough," Mr. Wyndham said gruffly. His fourth daughter wasn't above leaping onto the linen tablecloth and shimmying among the china and crystal place settings.

Mr. Daley entered the room and warmly greeted the Wyndhams, kissing each of the girls' cheeks in turn. Mrs. Daley's smile told him that he'd done the right thing by giving in to her wish to have the Wyndhams for Christmas Eve dinner.

The invitation was a reciprocation, as the Daleys had spent Thanksgiving with the Wyndhams. Mrs. Daley and Mrs. Wyndham had cooked up the holiday dinner plans to force their husbands into a grudging truce.

Mr. Wyndham had come to the Thanksgiving table for the wonderful meal his wife had prepared, but he'd spent the rest of the day on the deck, watching his breath condense in the air. He had seemed annoyed when Mr. Daley joined him shortly after dinner.

"I would like to apologize," Mr. Daley had said, "for my actions over the last several weeks."

"Don't sweat it," had been Mr. Wyndham's terse response.

"Reece seems well," Mr. Daley had said.

"Christopher took great care of her."

"Pardon me?" Mr. Daley had been surprised.

Mr. Wyndham had drained his beer and tossed the empty

can into the recycling bin near the back door. "Christopher is a good kid." Saying no more, he had wheeled himself into the house to catch the end of a football game.

"Good to see you again, Craig," Mr. Daley said, speaking to the man for the first time since Thanksgiving as he shook Mr. Wyndham's gloved hand. "Welcome to our home."

Mr. Wyndham, his hazel eyes narrowed, looked like he would rather be roasted alive in a gas fire than sitting in Daley manor.

Mrs. Wyndham flashed Mr. Daley a look of apology.

Mallory, her father's self-appointed assistant now that he wasn't communicating with his wife, took the handles of her father's chair. "There's a Christmas tree forest outside, Daddy. Come see it with me." She pushed him to the glittering wall of French doors facing the rear of the estate. Taryn and Bailey were already there, peering past the Christmas trees to get a glimpse of the snow-covered clay and grass tennis courts.

The two mothers watched the girls. "They look like princesses, Sara," Mrs. Daley said. "You really have beautiful daughters."

Mrs. Daley's gaze lingered on Kyle, who wore a white sweater and a black corduroy skirt. Kyle was only twelve but there was an ancient beauty about her that Mrs. Daley found alluring.

"Where's Christopher?" Mrs. Wyndham asked.

"He's, uh, still dressing, I imagine," Mrs. Daley said uncomfortably. She suddenly decided to busy herself with a poinsettia arrangement on the sumptuously decorated dining table.

"Is he doing any better?" Mrs. Wyndham asked softly.

Mrs. Daley smiled weakly. "He's not any worse. At least I can be thankful for that."

Christopher came into the room and found Reece standing before the fireplace. He placed his hands on her shoulders and brushed her ear with his nose as he said, "Merry Christmas Eve."

"Same to you," she smiled. She turned to face him. He wore

wool trousers, a dark blazer, and a shirt and tie. "You look nice. Very grown up."

"Reece, you look…" There were no words to describe how pretty she was in her simple black dress.

"Thank you," she blushed, accepting the silent compliment. She leaned in to whisper, "This is the one you picked out for me."

"Now I wish I hadn't missed so many dress-up days."

"Stop it, you're embarrassing me."

He would have gone on embarrassing her if Bigelow hadn't announced dinner.

Christopher escorted Reece to the table. He seated her and Taryn before seating himself. Bailey and Mallory giggled as Bigelow and another butler pulled chairs for them and their sisters.

Kelsey tapped one of the butlers on the arm. "Could I get a bell to ring to indicate when I want something?"

Reece would have kicked her under the table if her legs had been long enough to reach that far. The Daley's dining room table seemed as wide and long as a football field compared to the Wyndhams' cozy little drop-leaf.

Taryn nudged Reece with her elbow, and nodded toward Reece's plate.

A daisy sat on it.

Christopher had given her one fresh daisy every day without fail since Halloween. She would find it in her locker one day, and propped on her book bag in the senior lounge the next. She found them on her desk in homeroom, tucked into her gym locker, even resting on her pillow at home. Of all the honors, awards and tokens she had ever received, Christopher's daisies meant more to her than anything.

"It's so nice to have a table full of young people," Mr. Daley said as the last course was cleared from the table. "This room has never been filled with so much laughter."

Pride gleamed in Mrs. Wyndham's eyes as she gazed at her

daughters. That light dimmed when her eyes found her husband, who had rebuffed every effort to draw him into conversation. Mr. Wyndham sat between Taryn and Mrs. Daley. Although he was opposite his wife, he hadn't looked at her at all during dinner.

Before dessert was served, Mr. Daley offered Mr. Wyndham the opportunity to make a toast. He passed, so Mr. Daley took the task upon himself. He stood, and nodded toward Bigelow.

The house manager smartly clapped his gloved hands, and four butlers in black tails and white gloves carried in trays bearing bottles of Dom Perignon and crystal champagne flutes.

"Champagne!" Kelsey squealed. "This is awesome!"

Christopher stiffened, his eyes drawn to the star of light glinting off the deep green glass of a champagne bottle.

"Can we have some, Mom, please?" Bailey asked, her hands clasped beneath her chin. "I've never had champagne before, and this is a special occasion."

Mr. Daley spoke for the first time all night. "Special or not, you're still underage."

"I wasn't going to allow the girls champagne, Craig," Mrs. Wyndham said.

"The girls are being served sparkling white grape juice," Mr. Daley assured him.

Mr. Wyndham ignored both of them.

Reece looked at Christopher, who sat opposite her, and she noticed the beads of perspiration dotting his face. He had suddenly gone very pale.

A tall, heavy-set butler approached Christopher. His light brown hair was slicked back. It was long and brushed his collar. He smiled, revealing gold-plated upper teeth.

Christopher shut his eyes and bit back a scream. When he opened his eyes, the butler was at the head of the table presenting Mr. Daley with a glass of champagne. In the light at the head of the table, the butler's hair looked more blond than brown, and it barely touched his collar. His front teeth were as white as pearl.

Christopher panted and rubbed his eyes. The room felt too

close and too warm, and he loosened his tie so he could breathe a bit more freely.

Mr. Daley cheerfully lifted his glass. "To our children, our continued good health, and friendship."

A bubbling glass of champagne was placed before Christopher. He jumped back and bumped into the butler, knocking the champagne bottle onto the polished marble floor. It exploded in a noisy wet mess. He stood up and skirted around the broken bottle as though the pieces would skitter after him.

"Christopher, please take your seat," Mr. Daley said firmly.

"Chris?" Reece reached for him.

The room was spinning. Christopher couldn't meet any of the eyes staring at him. The scent of the champagne stung his nose and the clatter of the bubbles popping as they hit the air battered his ears. Laughter and screams echoed in his head.

"Christopher!" Mr. Daley shouted.

He ran from the room.

Ignoring her father's shouts, Reece ran after him.

They drove for close to two hours.

When Christopher ran into the garage and hopped into his car, Reece had joined him, no questions asked. She had sat silently beside him, even when he exited I-55 at Route 33 more than an hour later. He drove along the darkened, snowy roads as though he'd grown up in Juniper Falls.

He parked in front of an old house. The yellow, two-story farmhouse was half buried in snow. It had snowed almost every day for the past two weeks, and the weight of it had collapsed the roof over the porch. Jagged, broken edges of wood jutted into the night. The house looked like it had a mouthful of uneven fangs as Christopher kicked the debris aside and forced open the front door.

Reece followed him only because she was more frightened to stay outside by herself.

The electricity had been disconnected. The moonlight

filtering through the broken windows provided enough illumination for them to find their way. Christopher led her past an overturned sofa and a wall spattered with rifle shot. They climbed fifteen narrow steps to the room at the top of the steep staircase. The door gaped open, but none of the light from downstairs reached past the doorstop. Familiar dark filled the room.

Christopher walked into it, pulling her along with him.

"You've been here before," she said, her hand slipping from his.

"So have you."

"I should have said you've been here since." She was drawn toward the ray of moonlight in the bathroom. The pale light spotlighted a big, black stain on the floor. Reece cupped her elbows and shivered, and not entirely because of the cold. She stood in the doorway between the two rooms to be as close as possible to the one source of light.

"I came here the day after Halloween, but I just sat in the driveway. I came back again two weeks after that. I managed to get out of the car that time. This is the first time I've actually come into the house. And into this room."

She drew her shoulders in tighter. She didn't want to touch anything, not even the splintered doorframe.

"It still stinks," he said.

She detected a very faint, very unpleasant smell, a mixture of mildew and something rotten. "Let's go, Chris. I don't like this."

"Ross Liggett was an amateur boxer," he said. His voice came from the darkest corner of the room. "He spent three and a half years in prison for involuntary manslaughter. He cold-cocked a guy in a parking lot, and the guy died. A week before Ross was to be released from prison, he sexually assaulted his cell mate. Six months were added to his sentence, but he was released a month and a half early for good behavior.

"Gentry Liggett had about ten diagnosed learning disabilities and emotional problems. He wet the bed until he was fourteen. His medical records show sixteen visits to various emergency rooms, all between the ages of four and twelve. His left arm was broken four times.

"Their mother, Ardelia Liggett, died eleven years ago in this house, after a fall down the stairs. Emory Liggett, their father, was killed seven years ago in a freak accident at the auto plant that closed down a few years ago. Ross was nineteen and Gentry was twelve. Ross was working at the plant that day, and there were rumors about how the accident happened, but nothing was ever proven. One thing was for sure, though. Gentry never had to go to another emergency room."

"You know just a little too much about them." She took a half step into the dark room.

"D.I.I.'s computers put the world at your fingertips."

"They're dead now, Chris."

"That isn't good enough," his said, his voice rising. "I want them to pay for what they did to me. To both of us."

"Nothing worse can happen to them."

"That's not enough!" he yelled, suddenly swinging a rusty folding chair at the boarded window.

The chair crashed through the molding wood and fell into a snowdrift. A swirl of glittering snowflakes danced into the room on a rush of cold air and a wide beam of clear, bright moonlight.

Panting, Christopher stood in the wash of light. "I almost killed you," he started, moving toward her. "After you fell asleep, on that last night. Ross and Oliver had been laughing and talking about you and what they wanted to do to you. They were so drunk they could barely walk, but I know they would have done the things they talked about. Ross said he and Gentry might as well have some fun with you before they got rid of you. Oliver said he didn't care what they did, as long as your body was dropped off at the fountain on schedule."

"I put my hands on you, like this." He wrapped his hands around her neck, his thumbs crossing over her windpipe. "I knew they were going to kill me. If you had to die, too, I didn't want it to come at their hands.

"I squeezed my hands together." Tears shimmered in his eyes and his thumbs caressed her satiny skin. "You didn't move.

Were you so used to dying that you didn't mind that I was…that I would've…"

She gently gripped his wrists, but made no effort to remove his hands.

"You took my wrists, just like you're doing now." His voice shook. "You didn't move. I didn't know if you were awake or asleep, but you didn't move, like you trusted me to do the right thing."

He took her in a desperate embrace. "I couldn't do it. And I couldn't figure out a way to use your nail clippers to do it to myself and leave you all alone to face them in the morning. I sat there all night, holding you, listening to you breathe. When the sun came up, and it started getting lighter, I wanted to see the sun one last time. I wanted to feel fresh air on my skin. I thought of another way to use your nail clippers. Once I got the louvers off, I saw how big the hole was, and I knew you could get away."

She held him closer, wishing that she could click her heels three times and transport them someplace warm and sunny and far, far away. But there was no magic that could get them out of Juniper Falls until they faced the ghosts that repeatedly drew Christopher to the farmhouse.

"I want it to go away. I have so many wounds that haven't healed. I look at you and Bigelow, and I can't stop thinking about it. I can't stop feeling it."

Reece spoke to him, but the voices of dead men filled Christopher's ears.

"…*Lookit that, he bleeds red just like everybody else!*"

"*Don't! If he bleeds to death we won't get the money.*"

"…*Hold 'im, hold his shoulders, Gentry!*"

"*Damn, I think he likes it. You like champagne, don'tcha, boy?*"

"*Ever' time your ol' man looks at you, he's gonna see we screwed him the way he screwed Les.*"

"*I don't want to kill you, Christopher. I just want you to wish you were dead.*"

"*Miss Reece shor' looks peaceful…*"

"*We'll get 'er in the mornin'.*"

"Both of us?"

"Do you wish you were dead, Christopher?"

He staggered away from Reece, clapping his hands over his ears.

"Do you wish you were dead?!"

"Yes!" he cried. "Kill me! Please, please, kill me!"

She caught him as his knees buckled, his weight carrying them to the floor. Agonized sobs tore from him as he sat back on his heels, his hands over his ears.

"Chris," she said, a tremble in her voice, "it's okay. It's okay." She rose on her knees to hug him, to hold him close enough to force out his haunts.

"I'm here." She cupped his face and kissed the wet tracks of his tears. "Chris, I'm here."

He clutched at her waist. He moved his head slightly and Reece's lips caught his. He kissed her with sudden, shocking urgency.

She was imprisoned by the new and exhilarating sensations his touch sent through her veins and across every nerve. His hands, his kisses seemed to be everywhere at once, heating her skin as if she'd coated herself in baby oil and basked in the sun for two hours. He kissed her cheeks and her eyes, moistening his lips with her tears as his blazer slid from his shoulders.

They bared their scars to the winter night. She lay on their discarded clothing and he blanketed her, seeking solace within the confines of her body. Her name became the holiest of prayers, the one tether holding his soul to this world.

"Chris," she gasped, her thighs falling wide in response to the tender beckoning of his hands.

"Chris," she moaned, her clutching fingers digging into the meat of his shoulders.

"Chris!" she cried as he gained entry.

She cried out once again, and the sound carried through the cold air. He wanted to stop, he would have, but his need of her was too great. He sobbed her name once more, before falling beside her. They held each other, weeping quietly as they shivered in the light.

He touched the shimmering, sheer lapis blue film of her bra as she fastened it on. His hands were still shaking as he handed her the matching panties.

"These look familiar." He wouldn't meet her eyes.

She gave him a tiny smile. "I kept the Victoria's Secret stuff. Apparently, there are laws against returning underwear."

"I'm sorry." He finally looked at her.

"It's okay. I wanted to keep them. I usually get my underwear at Wal-Mart."

"I don't mean about that. I'm sorry about bringing you here, and...what we did."

He looked so vulnerable sitting cold and naked in the moonlight. She picked up his shirt and boxers and gave them to him. "Get dressed before you catch pneumonia." She pulled her dress on, and slipped her feet into her shoes. There was no point in putting her pantyhose back on. They were damaged beyond repair.

He slowly dressed. His hands were so shaky, Reece had to help him with his buttons.

"I really am sorry," he said.

"I could have stopped you, if I'd wanted to. You know that."

"It shouldn't have been like this." He was sickened by what he'd done. "It shouldn't have been here. It shouldn't have happened at all. You wanted to be with someone you loved, not—"

She touched her finger to his lips. "It was. I am." She smiled, and it was so beautiful that it very nearly exorcised his demons once and for all. "Let's go home."

Chapter Twenty-One

Sheriff Tatum sat in his truck and watched as Christopher helped Reece across the snowy porch of the Liggett house. He waited until they drove off in the tiny black sports car before he got out of the truck and entered the house the same way they had exited.

Silver light spilled from the room at the top of the stairs, and he went upstairs to investigate.

A tiny pool of black just outside the rectangle of moonlight on the floor caught his eye and he went into the room to examine it, his skin prickling just the littlest bit. Old Joss Ackles and his wife had called him a little while ago to say that the ghosts were screamin' at the Liggett place. He had come out expecting to find the wind rattling through a loose shutter or a boarded window.

He hadn't expected to find Christopher Daley III and Reece Whyndham.

Or a sheer black stocking.

He dropped the hosiery back in the moonlight and went downstairs. He stood in the living room and lit a big fat cigar. Instead of shaking the match out, he touched it to the sofa. The dry, cheap fabric whooshed into flame as he left the house.

He sat behind the wheel of his truck, watching the flames dance throughout the lower floor of the house. No surviving relatives had appeared to claim the house after Ross and Gentry died. C. August Daley II had purchased the property and its outbuildings and donated it to the town of Juniper Falls.

Sheriff Tatum figured that no one would mind if the building was destroyed by fire. It would certainly save razing costs. The Juniper Falls Development Committee—comprised of himself, Doc Soames, Mayor Chuck Ellerman, and Dixie Lee Campbell of Dixie's Luncheonette—had agreed that the Liggett farm would be the ideal site for the tentatively named Juniper Falls Technical Institute.

Christopher kissed Reece's cheek after he said goodnight. With both of their fathers nagging them, she had to pry his fingers from hers to join her family in her father's van. She didn't want to leave him, but there was no way she could stay, not with both their fathers angry enough to bite the heads off cobras.

The Daleys saw the Wyndhams off as the blue van crept toward the front gate. The instant the van turned the corner, Mr. Daley turned on Christopher. "Your behavior tonight was completely unacceptable! You storm out during dinner and don't return until nearly midnight? What could you possibly have been thinking?"

"Anything could have happened to you out there, Christopher," Mrs. Daley added anxiously. "You drove so fast that Ingo and Funaki couldn't keep up with you. You are never to leave this house without your bodyguards, you know that!"

Christopher ran up a flight of wide marble stairs and into the house. He ran across the gleaming cypress floors and up the winding staircase. His parents followed behind him, yammering about inconsideration and thoughtlessness.

"Just tell us why, Christopher," Mrs. Daley pleaded. "What possessed you to run off like that? I thought things were going rather well tonight."

Christopher had seemed almost normal. Through dinner he had smiled and laughed and talked with the Wyndham girls. He had been more relaxed and charming than she'd ever thought him capable. He'd kept his razor-edged sarcasm in check, and he'd bypassed every opportunity to be a smartass. He had changed in the past few months, but the change had been for the better, until this disappearing act.

Christopher sat on the foot of his bed. "What happened after you came to get me in Juniper Falls?"

Mrs. Daley looked to her husband for support.

Mr. Daley gritted his teeth. "Must we discuss this now, Christopher?"

Mrs. Daley rushed to her son's side. "Let's talk about it in the morning. A good night's sleep will do wonders for you."

"I want to go away." Christopher stood and stepped off the platform supporting his bed. "I need to get away from it."

"As you well know, that is out of the question!" Mr. Daley yelled.

"I can't stay here!" Christopher bellowed. He marched over to the authentic Tiffany lamp on one of his nightstands. "Who replaced this? When Ross and Gentry Liggett took me, I kicked this lamp over and smashed it to hell, but when I came home from the hospital, my room had been put in order as if nothing happened. Something happened here, Dad. Awful things happened to me, and everywhere I turn, everywhere I go, I see it. I need some peace!"

He sank into a leather chair, propped his elbows on his knees and clutched handfuls of his hair.

"Running from your problems will not solve them, Christopher," Mr. Daley said impatiently. "You are safe here. Those men are dead. They will never harm you again."

"You don't know what they did to me!" he screamed.

Mr. Daley responded coolly. "Yes, I do. I know exactly what they did to you."

"W-What's going on," Mrs. Daley asked. "Augie? Christopher?" She looked from her husband to her son. "What's this about?"

Mr. Daley stared at the ornate design of Christopher's vaulted ceiling. "There was a second video. I received it via inter-office mail the day after Leighton Oliver's suicide. I could only assume that Oliver expected to be ten million dollars richer and deep in hiding by the time I viewed it."

Mrs. Daley's legs went weak. She sat heavily on Christopher's bed.

"Christopher," Mr. Daley said miserably, "what did you do to make them want to hurt you so terribly?"

Christopher felt as if he were blacking out. A second video…he vaguely remembered Gentry's gleeful operation of his cell phone camera. He remembered Oliver grabbing him by the hair and lifting his face for it, ordering him to say hello to his parents.

Mr. Daley brought his fist to his mouth. He had watched the tape, as much of it as he could stand, right there in his office at The Janus while Christopher was in a bed at St. Mary's.

I don't want to kill you, Christopher. I just want you to wish you were dead.

In the brightest light of day, in the middle of the most important board meetings, those words haunted Mr. Daley. He faced his son, and he saw that Oliver's last wish was coming true.

"This will pass, son." Mr. Daley laid a hand on Christopher's shoulder. "Everything will return to normal, in time."

He threw his father's hand off. "I was born!" he sobbed. "That's what I did to make them hurt me! I did everything you ever told me to do. I followed your stupid rules. You know what they did to me? You know? And you still think I'll just forget about it?"

Christopher allowed his mother to take him in her arms, to press his head to her chest. He was bigger than she, but she managed to cradle him as she had when he was a much smaller, much happier boy.

"We'll get you some help," she cooed. "We'll find a way to get through this. If you want to go away, then you can go. You can go to Paris or New York City. Perhaps it would be best for you to get away from the house and school, and Reece."

He tensed.

"Perhaps your father was right all along. We should have kept you away from her. Reece is a wonderful girl but she's the strongest reminder of everything that happened."

He pulled out of her embrace, bumping into a floor lamp with a priceless Tiffany shade. The lamp tipped over and shattered explosively, casting that part of the cavernous room into darkness. "Leave me alone," he mumbled, a chilling deadness in his voice. "Please. Go away."

That was the one thing they could readily do for him, and they reluctantly left him in the shadows.

Taryn sat on the edge of the bathtub. The soft swell of her lower belly was starting to show, even in her loosest clothing. She dipped a fat pink sponge in the bath water before running it over Reece's back. "It's past midnight," Taryn said. "It's a little late for a bubble bath."

"Did Mom send you in here to tell me that?" Reece leaned against the back of the tub. She slid down until only her head, shoulders and knees were above the billowy suds skimming the water.

"Nope. She's busy filling our stockings." Taryn moved to sit on the lid of the toilet.

Every year Mrs. Wyndham faithfully filled the six stockings over the fireplace, and every Christmas morning they woke up to a living room full of gifts, and big red stockings stuffed with oranges, apples, nuts, candy canes, chocolates, cookies and earrings or bracelets.

"I'm glad you moved back home," said Reece. "It wouldn't have seemed like Christmas if you hadn't been here."

"Stirling planned for us to spend the holiday in Cancun. I'm sure he found someone to use my ticket. Hopefully, he'll get a quickie divorce down there, and save me the trouble of hiring a lawyer up here."

"Shouldn't you be getting some sleep? Mom said that you should be getting as much rest now, while you can."

"I thought you might want to talk."

Reece watched a clump of suds slide down her knee. "About what?"

Taryn stroked her sister's hair. "I don't know. You seemed a little funny when Christopher brought you back to the mansion."

Reece rubbed her nose.

"Where did you go?"

"Juniper Falls." Reece shivered even though she was immersed in warm water. Speaking the name of the town was enough to give her a scare, even in the familiar, brightly lit bathroom.

"Why?" Taryn asked, aghast. "What could you two have possibly been doing there?"

Reece stared straight ahead at the sparkling white tiles lining the wall.

A possible answer dawned on Taryn. "Reece…you guys didn't…did you?"

"Yes, we did."

"How could you be so stupid? A rich guy can give you a disease or knock you up just as easily as any other guy. You weren't exactly Christopher's first partner, either."

"He always uses protection," Reece argued weakly.

"Did he wear a condom this time?"

Reece answered with silence.

"It only takes one time to get pregnant, Reece."

"Really?" Reece said facetiously.

"I know you don't want a lecture but you have to be smarter than that next time."

"There won't be a next time," Reece said firmly. "Not until I'm married."

"Why did you do it this time?"

Reece rubbed one wet shoulder against her ear. "It just happened."

Taryn snorted.

"Really," Reece insisted. "He was so upset. He was scared and hurt and lonely and…lost. I would have done anything to make him feel good again."

"Sex is not therapy," Taryn said.

"I know, and I told you. It won't happen again."

Taryn patted her abdomen. "Famous last words."

Reece sponged water over her head and washed her face.

"How was it?" Taryn handed Reece a towel to dry her ears.

Reece spent a moment thinking before she said, "It was too much. Like I was feeling too much in too many places all at once. It made me dizzy, and I felt like I couldn't breathe. It hurt at first, a lot, but that passed quickly. Just when I started to feel really connected to Christopher, it was over. Do you know what I mean? Is that how it was supposed to be?"

"Yes. No. Yes and no, to both questions."

"Was it that way your first time?"

Taryn gave Reece a bath towel. Reece stood up and wrapped herself in it before stepping out of the tub. She sat on the lid of the toilet and let Taryn dry her hair for her.

"It was in the back of the limo on the way to our wedding reception," Taryn said. "As soon as the driver pulled away from the church, Stirling told me that he'd waited long enough, and that he couldn't wait another minute. I wanted him as much as he wanted me. I thought it would be this tumultuous, romantic experience that would leave me in a swoon or something."

Taryn exchanged the towel for a comb, and ran it through Reece's damp hair. "He pushed me back onto the seat and threw my skirt over my head. Two minutes later, he was done and I was bleeding on my slip. It was awful.

"I thought it would get better, and it did, a few times. But for the most part, our sex life has been awful. I'm sorry your first time wasn't better."

"It wasn't all bad. The worst part was how much it hurt at first," Reece said. "And how Christopher cried afterwards. He was so sorry. I'm not sorry at all."

"That's good," Taryn said warmly. She hugged Reece. "But you still shouldn't have done it without protection."

Kyle opened the back door and stepped out of the kitchen. Her father's wheelchair had cut neat tracks in the thin cover of snow on the floor of the deck. Kyle's tiny slippered footsteps followed the tracks to where her father sat at the railing, staring into the backyard.

"Merry Christmas, Daddy." She kissed his cold cheek, and slid a heavy gift onto his lap before going back into the warm house.

His neck stiff with cold, Mr. Wyndham looked down at the package. He wore gloves but the fingertips had been cut off, enabling him to maintain a good grip on his wheels. With numb fingers, he carefully removed the tape and wrapping paper Kyle had labored to make perfect.

He thought it was a book, and it was, but like no other book he had ever seen. He opened the padded leather cover. On the first wide page, beneath a sheet of plastic, was a yellowed piece of paper covered with his handwriting:

> *Dear Mom,*
>
> *Sorry I didn't write sooner. With school and work I haven't had a whole lot of time to write or call. (Sorry about missing your birthday. Happy belated 51st!)*
>
> *Another reason I've been busy is because I've met a girl. Her name is Sara Fairfield. She is studying to become a teacher and she is a very good cook. She makes the best apple pie and pot roast that I have ever had. (Yours is better so don't worry, but Sara's is really good, too.) She has black hair, brown eyes and the best set of gams God ever made. Tell Dad. (Just kidding.) I wish I was a poet so I could really tell you exactly how beautiful she is. She's really nice, too. She smiles all the time and she has the best laugh. It sounds like a symphony of angels.*
>
> *We met last week at Homecoming. Sara was at the refreshment stand. She made double-chocolate chip cookies to raise money for her friend's sorority. She's so sweet that way.*
>
> *I know you will think I'm crazy, but it really was love at first sight. When you meet Sara, you'll love her too. I'm bringing her home for Thanksgiving. I haven't asked her yet, but I know she'll say yes. I think she likes me a lot, too.*
>
> *I will call you in a few days. Thanks again for the check, and for the socks.*
>
> Love,
Craig

The thirty-year-old letter had been written during his freshman year at the University of Maryland at College Park. He read it over and over, only vaguely wondering how Kyle had gotten her hands on it.

The letter was followed by a photograph of him and Sara standing beside his father's Chrysler station wagon. The picture was as old as the letter. His mother had taken it right before his father had driven them back to College Park after the Thanksgiving holiday.

He touched the plastic film over Sara's face. God, she was beautiful, even bundled up in a heavy parka and a wool cap that hid her gorgeous hair. And he had been right. His parents had loved her.

More letters and pictures followed. There were love letters that he and Sara had written to each other shortly after graduation, when she was in Virginia caring for her sick father and he was at the fire academy.

There were pictures from their wedding and honeymoon. He laughed when he came to a photo of Sara, nine months pregnant with Taryn, on her hands and knees sanding the floor of their first apartment in Baltimore.

There were notes, birthday cards, birth announcements and baby photos. There were pictures of the girls at christenings and first communions, at recitals and graduations, accepting trophies and breaking tapes.

Kyle had compiled the highest, most special moments of his life.

The last photo in the book was a digital shot of the girls that Sara had taken right before they went to the Daleys for Christmas Eve dinner. The girls were dressed up for their first visit to a mansion. They were lovely.

The last page in the book was conspicuously empty, as though Kyle had been unsure of what should or would come next. A photo of her father alone in the snow on the patio? A photo of Sara alone in the kitchen?

His wife and daughters, his life, sat on his lap.

He closed the book and hugged it to his chest. The warmth of what had gone into creating the book, the life it contained, seeped into him, melting the shell of ice encasing his heart. His shoulders heaved as the ice turned to water and left him in the form of tears.

Christmas had always been a day of laughter and fun, thanks to the effort Sara put into it. They had no money for a wealth of gifts but Sara always made each Christmas memorable.

This year, the house was so quiet. Taryn wasn't barking orders at her sisters. Reece wasn't arguing with Bailey. Kelsey wasn't dancing. Mallory wasn't singing. And Kyle. His baby, Kyle, wasn't sitting near his chair or in the kitchen, reading or drawing.

He covered his eyes, ashamed of how cruelly he had treated his wife and how selfish he had been toward his own children. He wondered if his family would ever forgive him.

He didn't have to wonder for long.

"Craig?"

He lifted his head at the sound of his wife's voice.

"Kyle said you wanted to see me?"

She sounded so hesitant, almost afraid. *I made her feel that way,* he thought despondently. "I do," he said, speaking to his wife without rancor for the first time in months. Kyle was always right, although how she knew to send her mother out at that very moment, he would never know.

Mrs. Wyndham kneeled at his side, her chenille robe pooling at her knees, and glanced at the book in his lap. Tears sprang to her eyes, and when they coursed down her cheeks, her husband tenderly brushed them away with his thumb.

"Mallory's running a bath for you." She clasped his hand to her cheek. "Kyle said you wanted to take a hot bath before you opened the rest of your presents."

Once again, Kyle was right. "I love you, Sara," he said, meaning it with his whole heart.

"I love you, too." She smiled through her tears, cherishing the words he hadn't spoken to her in so long.

"I'm sorry." He held her face in his hands and kissed her. "I'm so sorry for behaving like a complete idiot."

"I know." She kissed his hands and his face. "The girls know, too."

He pulled her onto his lap and hugged her. Their daughters watched from the kitchen window. "It's about time," Kelsey said. "Daddy was so bummin' me out."

Chapter Twenty-Two

"Open mine next, Dad." Mallory handed her father a slim flat box wrapped in green and gold paper. Mr. Wyndham opened the gift and held up the new leather gloves.

"These are great, sweetheart," he said.

The fingerless padded gloves fit perfectly. The thick leather would last a long time, no matter how much wheeling he did in them. He cupped Mallory's cheek. The way she looked at him would have started his tears again if Bono hadn't leaped onto his lap and whimpered with jealousy.

"That is the most selfish dog I have ever seen," Taryn said. "He thinks he's the only one in this house who should get any attention."

Kelsey scooped Bono up and kissed the dog's dreadlocked head. "You'll find out about selfish when my niece is born. There's nothing greedier than a baby."

"How would you know?" Taryn asked. She was lying on the sofa, suffering through morning sickness. "You've never had a baby. Have you?"

"No," Kelsey said over her family's laughter, "but I babysat the Kessler kid for two weeks last summer. I know about greedy."

"Timmy Kessler is a sweet baby," Kyle said. She had inherited the Kessler job when Kelsey quit. Kyle lightly snapped her fingers. Bono obediently squirmed out of Kelsey's arms and leaped into Kyle's lap.

"You know how to handle Timmy," Kelsey charged, her hands on her hips. She was baffled by the way Bono responded instantly to Kyle's every command.

The phone rang, and Reece, Bailey, Mallory and Kelsey stampeded into the kitchen to answer it. The runner reached it first. "It's for me!" Reece cried triumphantly, shooing her sisters out of the kitchen with a regal wave of her hand.

"Reece?" It was Mrs. Daley. "Forgive me, for disturbing you. I'm sure you're enjoying the holiday with your family."

"It's not a problem," Reece said curiously. "Is everything

okay?"

"No. I'm afraid it's not."

Reece leaned heavily against the wall, anxiously twisting the phone cord.

"Christopher is having some sort of, uh, breakdown. I was hoping you could help us. Please."

"I'll be right there."

"Thank you," Mrs. Daley said. "Thank you, Reece."

"Why is this happening to him?" Reece asked her father, who had insisted on driving her to Daley Manor. "He was so strong for me when we were in Juniper Falls. They couldn't touch him, not on the inside..." The answer hit her no sooner than the words left her mouth. She knew exactly why he was falling apart.

Mr. Wyndham drove west on Layton Rd. "Remember how I was after my accident," he said. "I struck out at everyone. All the hurt and anger I felt, I unleashed on everyone around me. Christopher seems to have turned it inward, on himself. In some ways it's harder for him than it was for me. What happened to me was an accident. It was my fault. I knew I shouldn't have gone back into that building, but I went in anyway. I made a mistake and I'm still coming to terms with it. What happened to Christopher was on purpose. That makes it harder to rationalize."

Reece followed Mrs. Daley through the enormous house that seemed more like a museum than a home. They paused at the massive door to Christopher's suite.

"He never came down for breakfast," Mrs. Daley explained. "I came up for him. I opened the door and the room was so dark, I had to turn on the light to see him. He screamed. He jumped out of his bed and ran away from me. I'm his mother, and he ran from me."

Reece stepped ahead of Mrs. Daley and opened the heavy

oak door. The room looked as big as her whole house. It had vaulted ceilings and ornate furniture made of some highly polished dark wood. Six pairs of French doors lined one wall, but heavy brocade draperies closed out the bright Christmas morning.

Reece moved farther into the room, to Christopher's bed. She stepped onto the platform and lightly touched one of his pillows, which bore the faint impression of his head. She ran her hand along the soft, cool bed sheet, wondering how it felt to sleep all alone in such a huge room.

"He wasn't running from you," Reece said, gazing at the wall of draperies.

"I don't understand this behavior," Mrs. Daley said. "He's so fearful. He hides out in this dark room all of the time."

"Our monsters came out in the light. We were safe in the dark. Where is he?"

Mrs. Daley seemed embarrassed as she led Reece to another room. She placed her hand on the door. "It's voice-controlled," she said before tearfully excusing herself.

There were no knobs or handles on the door. "Open?" Reece said softly, feeling slightly stupid. The doors slid apart and the track lighting came on, drenching the two-room chamber in artificial sunlight. She stepped into the room and heard a gasp and the muted rustle of movement over the thick carpet.

"Close." The doors came together behind her and the light went off. She blindly felt her way past drawers with glass windows and rows of jackets, shirts, and trousers hanging above them. The rooms smelled faintly of cedar. "I can't find you." She thudded against a wall of shoes.

"I'm here."

She dropped to her hands and knees and crawled beneath a row of long wool coats. She bumped into him. He grabbed her and pulled her into his arms. He held her as though he were afraid she would disappear. She stroked his hair and comforted him as he had once comforted her.

"They keep telling me to put it behind me," he said. "I can't, not until I have the whole thing."

"I know. I'm missing pieces, too."

"What happened after you got away? My parents won't tell me. But I need to know."

"Everything happened so fast once I got to the luncheonette." She held him closer. "Sheriff Tatum and his deputies got in their trucks and took off. My legs were in some kind of shock and I couldn't walk. I was taken to Dr. Soames and I called my parents from his office. He had just finished stitching the cut on my leg when Sheriff Tatum and one of his deputies brought you in.

"The doctor's office was really small. There were only two exam tables separated by a curtain. I was on one table and they put you on the other. There was fresh blood splattered all over you, and I freaked out, but then Sheriff Tatum said it was Gentry Liggett's. He said Gentry tried to shoot you, so he had to fire on him. He found out later that Gentry's gun had no bullets. Leighton Oliver was an idiot, but I guess he wasn't dumb enough to give Gentry a loaded gun.

"Dr. Soames called for a MediFlight to St. Louis, but your dad's helicopter got there first. Your dad really went nuts. He demanded to know Dr. Soames's qualifications and accused him of being a 'hick veterinarian.' Everyone was crying. You were fading in and out of consciousness. Dr. Soames came with us in the helicopter, to monitor you. He didn't think you'd make it to St. Louis.

"Once we landed at St. Mary's Hospital, you were rushed off to one place, I was taken to another. I fell asleep as soon as I hit a bed. I woke up later that day as my mom was giving me a sponge bath. She told me that you'd had surgery.

"I was dehydrated and in shock, so St. Mary's kept me until Friday morning. They monitored my heart, because of the shot from the stun gun. I tried to visit you, every day, but the guards outside your room wouldn't let anyone in.

"Your mom let me see you on Friday, before I went home. I couldn't get too close to you because there were so many machines connected to you. Your dad caught me there and he was so angry. He said everything would fall apart if anyone saw us together.

"I went to school on Monday. I lied to everybody and said that I'd been with my grandparents in Baltimore all week, visiting the Johns Hopkins campus. I tried to visit you again, but the guards had strict orders not to let anyone other than your mom and dad in to see you. Even when you were taken home I couldn't see you. That Hilda was a beast."

He trembled in her arms. She tugged down one of the heavy wool coats and covered him with it. They sat in the darkness for a long time before she said, "What haven't you told me?"

Burning sobs backed up in his throat and chest until they burst forth with his words as more missing pieces spilled from him in a torrent of anguish. He spared no detail of what Oliver and the Liggetts had done to him on that last night in Juniper Falls.

He told her what she knew already, about the burns, beatings, and cuts. And then he told her what she didn't know.

"It wasn't enough to make me cry. It wasn't enough to make me scream or bleed, or piss in my pants." He told her how they had held him down, how they had laughed as they filmed the atrocity Ross had committed upon him with an empty champagne bottle. The revelation tumbled from his lips in a painful jumble that left him empty of everything but sorrow.

"Yesterday, when we were in Juniper Falls," he stammered, "I wanted to forget. I thought what we did would make me feel normal again."

"Did it?"

Her voice was as gentle and soothing to his wounded spirit as a breath of spring air. "Yes. For a while."

"The pain will fade, Chris."

"No, it won't." His fingers curled tighter into her shirt. "Not until it kills me."

"The Liggetts couldn't kill you. Their memory won't kill you, either. I won't let it. You used yourself up protecting me. I realized that on the way over here. You got me through Juniper Falls, and my parents and my sisters were there for me when I came back. They cried with me. They helped chase away my nightmares. I was never alone. Neither are you, Chris. You have me. You'll get through this."

"I don't have your strength."

"You have more strength than I ever did. You took everything they dished out. That's your strength, Chris. You faced things head on, to protect me. I ran."

She suddenly stood. She grabbed his hand and pulled him up alongside her. "Where's the light switch?"

"Lights," he said.

They came on, and he flinched. The sight of her in jeans and a long sleeved T-shirt banished the terror-filled images the light conjured.

"Take a shower," she ordered.

She chose clothing for him while he bathed. She opened the drapes and tied them back, filling the room with sunlight. Christopher left the bathroom a few minutes later with a towel swathed about his hips. Mindless of her presence, he dropped his towel and pulled on the shorts she had selected for him.

She went to him, drawn by the faint patches of scar tissue on his chest and back. She had been too distracted the night before to see how well he had healed. This was her first glimpse of the scars that his pants had covered on that last morning in Juniper Falls.

He put on the rest of his clothes and looked at her. Only then did he notice that she was wearing a pair of his shorts.

Chapter Twenty-Three

He watched her as she guided him through a series of stretches out on the west veranda. If she was cold in his baggy shorts, she gave no indication of it. She smiled at him as she sat to do an inner thigh stretch and motioned for him to do the same.

He would have followed her to the end of time if she wanted him to. He was stretching along with her when Mr. Daley stormed out onto the veranda, Ingo and Funaki right behind him.

"What's the meaning of this?" Mr. Daley demanded, facing Christopher and ignoring Reece. "We agreed that you wouldn't see Reece anymore."

"We didn't agree on anything," Christopher said morosely.

"You will not defy me, Christopher," Mr. Daley said darkly.

Reece jabbed Mr. Daley in the left shoulder. He whirled to face her. "This has nothing to do with you, Reece," he said. "Please don't take this personally. Christopher's mother and I believe it would be in his best interest to separate himself from the things that remind him of his experience."

"Is that one of your stupid rules?" Reece asked. "Don't fight. Do what they say. Don't talk about how they hurt you. Don't think about it. Pretend it didn't happen? You want him to run away from it? Fine. That's exactly what he's going to do."

She took his hand and started running.

Ingo and Funaki followed for as long as they could before breathlessly falling far behind. It was a struggle but Christopher kept up with Reece's pace, running beside her until sweat poured down his face. They ran past the snowy gardens and the tennis courts, past the swimming pool and the stables. They ran past the lake and over the bridge spanning the stream bubbling through the Daley property. They ran into the woods.

Christopher put one foot in front of the other, his form much more awkward and labored than Reece's. They ran together, but their thoughts were as different as their styles of running.

Reece was completely at peace, lost in the rhythm of movement. Her last run had been weeks ago, through Juniper Falls. She easily fell into her familiar patterns of breathing and pacing. Christopher ran as though he were being chased. He was, only the things he ran from were trapped in his head.

He ran faster, his arms and legs pumping, his breathing ragged. The repercussion of each footfall traveled through his legs as he crunched through the undisturbed carpet of snow. The muscles of his shoulders and back burned as he ran harder and faster to keep pace with Reece.

He hadn't been able to run in Juniper Falls. He had been trapped, like an animal in a cage awaiting slaughter. His heart pounded with blood that felt like molten lead. He threw his arms wide as breathless screams of despair tore from his throat and filled the desolate woods. His fists struck out at phantoms. He fell, still fighting, still punching, still spitting curses, damning the Liggetts to hell. He screamed until his throat was raw, and he beat the ground and the bare trees until his hands bled.

Tears bleared his vision but he could see the dark chocolate of Reece's hair far ahead of him. He started running before he lost sight of her all together. He ran, putting one foot in front of the other, his arms pumping in concert with his knees. He left the ghosts behind as he focused on that bobbing spot of brown in the poplars.

He didn't have breath to spare to call her, so he ran, keeping her in sight. He ran, thinking only of her. Suddenly, his mind emptied. There was nothing but the blue sky above him, the snowy ground below him and the brisk Christmas air around him. There was no pain, not of his memories, not of his over-wrought body, not of the fight with his parents. There was only the surge of power within his body.

In that one moment of freedom, Christopher felt as if he could run forever.

Reece slowed and he caught up to her. She brought them to a walk, and he took her hand. They followed the stone wall bordering the north side of the Daley property, and it led them back to the manor.

Christopher's parents and bodyguards rushed onto the veranda when they spotted them.

"Augie, stop them!" Mrs. Daley cried when Ingo and Funaki started for Reece.

Ingo was a former Olympic boxer who had represented his homeland of Australia. Funaki, who had trained to be a sumatori until he failed to reach the height requirement, was a black belt in karate. Reece fearlessly faced the two hulks. When Ingo reached for her shoulder, she knocked his arm aside with a neat block that stung more than just a little bit.

Christopher stepped in Funaki's path. "I'm entitled to take a walk with my girlfriend." He turned to his father. "I'm not leaving town, Dad, and I won't stop seeing Reece."

"Christopher," Mr. Daley exhaled sharply, girding himself for another argument, "I love you and I will not stand for this willfulness. This running off has got to stop."

"What?" Christopher whipped his head toward Reece. Had she heard the same thing he had?

"I won't have you running off unprotected," Mr. Daley finished.

"Father, what did you say before that?" Christopher stepped onto the veranda. "Dad…please."

"I love you," Mr. Daley said humbly. "When I think of what those bastards did to you… I want to kill them all over again. I wish I could have protected you. Every time you leave the house for school, or to visit Reece, or to even walk the grounds, I can't think for dreading that it will be the time you don't return to me. I can't lose you, son. All I can do is protect you the very best I can."

"I don't need you to protect me from what's already happened," Christopher implored. "I need you to help me. I don't want to be so afraid anymore."

"We'll help you, darling," Mrs. Daley wept, cupping his face.

Christopher stepped away from his mother and studied his

father's face. He touched his father's cheek. "I'm not like you. I've never been powerful or strong. I'm sorry I'm so weak. I'm sorry I'm such a disappointment."

The hard lines in Mr. Daley's face softened. "Chris…is that what you think? That you're a disappointment to me?" He grabbed him and hugged him. "Son, nothing could be further from the truth. I'm the one who's weak. I'm the one who needed to live behind a lie. I wish I had even a fraction of your strength and courage.

"Shadows die in full light," Mr. Daley said. "So do lies. We'll get the help we need, Christopher. I promise."

He threw his arms around his father, who planted a kiss on his sweaty brow.

Epilogue

Tying the belt of the thick cotton robe around her middle, Reece left the bathroom. She felt as if she were walking on clouds as she padded barefoot across the thick white carpet and went onto the terrace. Christopher sat at a glass table in a stylized chair made of black leather and silver chrome. He wore a dark blue sports shirt, khaki shorts and hiking sandals.

Reece took the empty chair opposite him and smiled appreciatively at the breakfast of scones, clotted cream, fresh fruit and tea that he had ordered for them.

There was a daisy tucked into her napkin holder.

"Good shower?" He removed his Vuarnet sunglasses.

His eyes were the exact azure hue of the calm, sun-dappled water filling their view. "Awesome shower." She inhaled. She couldn't get enough of the salty pungency of the Mediterranean Sea.

"Good run?" he asked knowingly.

"Awesome run," she answered, blushing.

Of all the jewels he'd seen in his life, none were more beautiful than Reece's eyes.

"I met an Italian count who asked me to come away with him to his piazza in Rome."

He lifted his eyebrows. His deep tan made them look impossibly black. "Really?" he asked, knowing it was unlikely that she'd encountered anyone. They were on a private beach.

"No," she giggled.

This was the first morning in months that they hadn't run together. They ran every day, either before school on Prescott's track, or after school at Daley Manor. This was their first day of spring break and their first day on the Riviera, and Reece had wanted to take her morning run alone, to fulfill a modest dream.

"Maybe I should run with you tomorrow," he offered.

"I'd like that." She nibbled a cool, sweet slice of honeydew melon.

"Really?"

"Yes. Really."

"How shall I dress?" he asked slyly. "Or should I dress at all?"

Other than Christmas Eve, they had abstained from a sexual relationship. It was easy, really, because they shared an intimacy that went far beyond sex. He had assumed that he wouldn't see her full beauty again until after they were married. Once he asked her.

"I'll decide in the morning," she laughed, blushing all the way down to her toes.

He moved to her side of the table and dropped to one knee beside her chair. "Is the nightmare over?"

She bowed her head until her lips touched his hair. After brushing soft kisses over each of his eyes, she pressed her cheek to his head. He hugged her so tightly he almost lifted her from the chair. Everything looked so different now, so alive and bright in the light of the Italian sun.

Daily therapy sessions with Carol Livingston over the winter holiday break had started all of the Daleys and Wyndhams on the path to full recovery, and Christopher continued to see her on a weekly basis, with his father's blessing. He was healing. They all were.

"Yes," she said. "Right here and right now is what's real. We're wide awake now."

Author Biography

Crystal Hubbard was reared in St. Louis, Missouri, where she began her writing career in her seventh-grade French class at Busch Junior High School for Gifted Students. A former Boston newspaper reporter and sports copy editor, she is an award-winning author of picture books, contemporary and historical romance novels, and short stories. When she is not writing, she volunteers in classrooms, conducting reading and writing workshops and composing grant proposals for public school teachers. She is a dedicated advocate for United States veterans and active troops, and she campaigns every holiday season for the Marines Toys for Tots Foundation. Her hobbies include reading, sewing, cooking, traveling, boxing, hiking, and orchestrating harmless yet clever pranks. *Alive and Unharmed* is her second young adult novel. Her first young adult novel, *Million Dollar Girl* (which also takes place at the fictional Prescott High School) was written under the pseudonym Anne Wilde.

Made in the USA
San Bernardino, CA
09 March 2014